Evan had been alone for nearly fifteen minutes when the door opened and Eliza Tertia came in. He knew her at once by the pleasant vanillalike scent she wore.

"Sorry I'm late," she said as she got to work.

She looked at his chart, studied his meters, made entries in a ledger, then inspected a small black sphere, about the size of a handball, spinning on a pivot atop a small walnut box. There was an index number in a window, and she entered this figure on a chart. She seemed nervous.

Evan himself was trembling with anticipation. He felt fearful, yet happy, like the Friday night last fall when he had been sent in to play against a lineman who outweighed him by nearly forty pounds. His head told him he'd be demolished; his heart said, Charge!

Also available from
VAGABOND BOOKS

THE FOREVER FORMULA

by
FRANK BONHAM

Vagabond Books

SCHOLASTIC BOOK SERVICES
New York Toronto London Auckland Sydney Tokyo

*To William Campbell Gault,
my old friend and adviser—
though his advice is sometimes wrong,
his friendship is always right.*

ISBN 0-590-32305-9

12 11 10 9 8 7 6 5 4 3 2 1   6   2 3 4 5 6 7/8

Printed in the U. S. A.   06

There were three possible explanations for the strange and terrifying things that were happening to Evan Clark. The most likely, he thought, was that he had had an accident on his moped and suffered a brain concussion. But if that were true, why were there no bandages on his head? And yet there were no bumps or stitches, no physical evidence of any kind.

The second possibility — an even more chilling one — was that he was dying of a brain tumor. But again there were no clear indications, only bone-breaking chills and an endless repertoire of vivid hallucinations.

The third likelihood was that he had been given a hallucinatory drug, and that the whole experience was a bad dream. This dream, or hallucination, took the form of his being a patient in a strange and futuristic hospital, his body so cold that several times he actually thought he saw frost on his hands!

And the nurses! For in his fantasy he seemed to have three of them, three petite little women in powder blue coveralls, all named Eliza, and identical, with dark brown hair, gray eyes, and black lashes. They were about eighteen, and he could not distinguish one from another, except for a certain idiosyncrasy in his day nurse. This particular Eliza often wore perfume, which smelled like sugar cookies baking in his mother's kitchen, a warm and homey fragrance.

(And thanks a lot, Mom, he thought forlornly, for never coming to see me! You too, Dad.)

Another clue to his having more than one nurse was that when one took over for another, there would sometimes be two of them in the room for a few moments, two pretty little things as alike as two pennies.

Another of his hallucinations was "Iron Eyes," a weird creature who occasionally came to stare at him through a window in the door. Instead of eyes, this man — this creature — had large rotating metal orbs set in his eye sockets! They resembled a jeweler's vision of a wasp or fly's eyes, hundreds of glittering, black chips set in silver and capable of rotating in any direction. Evan shivered every time Iron Eyes stared at him.

Hold everything!

In his head he felt a familiar slipping of pulleys, the sensation that always preceded a glimpse of what he still thought of as reality. There was an instant of dizziness, a pressure in his ears, and then it seemed as though a cloud of steam parted and he had a vision of the real world. . . .

2

He saw a familiar face, with brooding dark eyes and the hooked beak of a hawk. Dr. Hawkins: something about him. Name like his nose. A dream about Hawkins, about his cabin in the woods, where Evan worked Saturdays. At the old missile silo he had bought from the government at auction.

A now-familiar dialogue began to run like a tape.
Evan?

Yes, sir.

Can I persuade you to forget about Mr. Kindred?

Yes. No. Something. . .

Why did you come down here?

The door of the silo was open and your station wagon was parked near it. The shed was locked and I couldn't get the lawnmower out, so I came down to look for you.

Hawkins' features grew clearer and sharper. He looked grave but determined.

I thought Mr. Kindred had drowned fishing, Doctor Hawkins. And they never found his body. That's what the paper said.

The vision thinned, and he could make out, through Hawkins' face, the meters and dials on the wall near his bed. (He had decided some time ago that they registered his vital signs, for there were needles that made squiggles in rhythm with his heartbeat, a digital counter that changed every time he took a breath, and clock faces that might record his blood pressure.)

Then the vision of Hawkins' glum features blotted out the meters again, a darker printout than ever before.

Yes, that's Mr. Kindred in there. But try to under-

*stand this, Moose. May I call you Moose? I know
your friends do, and I hope you consider me your
friend. Mr. Kindred was very, very ill. Dying. The
doctors said he had only a few days left. I could
bring him back even now, you see, but then he'd just
go on and die.*

Now, Moose, don't be frightened. No, please —!

Evan whimpered, and the memory disintegrated.
He was back in the hospital bed, watching his meters
go wild over the terrifying memory that had once
again eluded him like a forgotten name.

But all right.

He thought; therefore he was.

So what if he'd been doped?

Well, if that were the case, then he ought to hear
laughter soon. Someone had put a drug in his drink
and they were all watching his reactions. But he
didn't have friends like that. And, besides, he knew
in his heart that he had been in the hospital for days.
Knew it. Too much evidence that couldn't be explained away. Yet there was unassailable proof on
the other side, too. Bewildering! But if he were in the
hospital, why hadn't his parents come to see him?
Did that mean something terrible had happened to
his entire family? A plane crash or something?

He moaned. He could not bear to think about it.

Yet he was stronger this morning. Morning? The
digital plate over the door read 0820, and pinkish
light washed the window. Eliza Tertia was late
again. She was, in fact, assuming a distinctive per-
sonality. Only she was ever late; only she wore perfume. And she alone ever answered a question. So he
was beginning to focus his hopes on Eliza Tertia.
Tertia: funny name. From Latin I, he knew that

4

tertia meant "third," and his father had once mentioned, in one of his little asides, that Roman girls were all named after their mothers and given a number as a second name, such as Tertia or Octavia (eighth).

He was shrewd enough to know that if he were to get any information out of the nurses, it would be Tertia, who sometimes seemed almost human, and occasionally let slip something informative. Often more shocking than reassuring, however. For instance, the bomb she had dropped in his lap yesterday!

Going through her purse, she had paused to count her money, seeming troubled. Evan asked to see the strange-looking bank notes, and she hesitated but finally handed him a one-dollar bill.

A blue one!

And as if that were not enough, the portrait on it, in sepia, was not of George Washington — not in this hospital! — but of Walter Stevens Clark, his father!

Evan heard voices outside his door. Eliza Tertia (or Octavia, or Duodecima) glanced in at him. Suddenly he made a decision, so fast it took his breath, causing his meters to leap. He would surprise Eliza Tertia today. He was not quite as helpless as Iron Eyes, the guards, and the nurses thought. For although they left nothing sharp or heavy around for him to use as a weapon, he had a potential weapon they had overlooked.

A water glass.

With that ordinary water glass, he was going to work some magic that might shake Eliza Tertia to her toes, might finally get her talking. . . .

2

*E*liza Tertia hurried up the steps from the roaring subway hole and emerged on a broad sidewalk a block from Clark Memorial Hospital. Above this section of the city, as in certain others, there arched a grimy dome of plastic panes, like the roof of an arboretum, so that the air inside could be enriched and filtered. She restored herself with deep breaths of fortified air faintly tinged with pine scent, the first proper air she'd breathed since she went off duty at the hospital yesterday. But though she felt refreshed, her mood remained an anxious one.

Late again, Eliza! she thought in vexation. What is wrong with you?

Well, the subway incident — a Juvenile Underground terrorist had tried to bomb a train — had robbed her of a half hour. But the simple truth was that she had not allowed time for the inevitable pinches of crosstown travel. She lived in Harley Mansions, a dead city neighborhood, and every morning she had to take the subway to Dome Seven.

She had wasted time, too, in cooking that quaint twentieth-century treat her patient had asked for — something called a "dough nut." Nevertheless, such lack of time-planning was almost unheard of in a nurse-clone of the Eliza strain. Elizas were perfect.

So, late and anxious, she hurried along the sidewalk, a small-bodied figure in a pastel pink coverall, wearing a jaunty little leather cap. The neighborhood was a quiet one of elegant shops catering to very elderly people—Gold Seniors, a hundred and fifty plus. Snickeringly, they were referred to as Guppies, because of the translucency of their white faces and their pale salt-ball eyes. Above endless blocks of apartments rose the shining truncated pyramid of the hospital, gleaming in the morning like blue ice.

She passed a sidewalk cafe where, even at this early hour, a congregation of elderly people was seated at tiny tables drinking pink gin. Most of them had poodles dyed in pastel colors: pink, lavender, yellow. Some were playing dominoes, but the majority of them merely gazed blankly at the little nurse as she hurried by. An old man, at least two hundred, judging by the aspic translucency of his skin, waved at her and called,

"Hi, sweetie!"

Eliza smiled, fluttered her fingers at him, and looked the other way. Over on her right was a withered park, where other Guppies walked their poodles or played one of their endless, complex lawn games, which always ended in quarrels, with them and their dogs snapping at each other. Poor dears! thought Eliza.

Carrying her nurse's bag in one hand, a purse in the other, she crossed the street. She saw two other nurses approaching, both wearing off-duty coveralls like hers, but of different colors. She did not recognize them, since they were identical to all other clones of the Eliza strain, but guessed they were Eliza Duodecima and Eliza Octavia. Looking into the face of any other Eliza was like seeing herself in a mirror. Like herself, they were petite; but, unlike her, they wore their dark hair impishly curled. Today, just to surprise Evan, she had done hers up in the style of the marble bust of a Greek girl she had seen in a museum.

"Late again, Tertia!" one of them said, and laughed. "Colonel Jansen's having kittens."

"Somebody could have covered for me, Duo," Eliza reproached her. "Said I'd called in for a late pass, or — or something."

"Quinta used that one yesterday, Tertia. I'm Sexta, by the way. Have to mend your ways."

"The most terrible thing —!" Eliza began, but the others only giggled and looked at each other. They had heard her famous alibis before.

"Do tell," Sexta said, then pointed suddenly. "See that man? Maybe you can go in with him—get lost in the confusion. He's quite a celebrity. Worth trying. We got his autograph!"

Farther along, Eliza saw a burly figure in a gleaming shirt of metal fabric apparently waiting to be let into the hospital. He looked vaguely familiar.

8

"Looks too young for C.M.H.," she commented. "Who is it?"

" 'When you smell a rat, call Tuggey,' " trilled Sexta, just the way the girl did in the television commercial.

"The exterminator? But there *couldn't* be a rat in C.M.H. Aren't we vermin-proof?" She was shocked; it was enough to have to cope with the vicious things at home.

"Hope so," sighed Eliza Sexta. "Anyway, Jansen said we may all have to have the new fever shots. Tata!"

Eliza watched Captain Tuggey push the revolving door and enter, after picking up a small-animal cage. So much for the claim that Clark Memorial was proof against rats! she thought, with a sigh. She hurried on, but the revolving door had locked again by the time she reached the entrance. On one side of the door was a polished brass plaque with the hospital's name. On the other, also in brass, were the Latin words for "Never Say Die": *Non Fato Cedemus.*

Below the brass plaque, some Juvenile Underground person had painted the letters *EP*, and an elongated *S* with a dot in the upper curl, making it resemble an elephant's head. *EP* was Juvie shorthand for *Elephant Plan*, though no one knew for sure what *that* meant — just terrorist language for some new plot. It seemed she had begun to see the elephant-head graffiti on walls everywhere.

Eliza slipped her ID card into a slot and hurried inside when the revolving door began to turn. She presented herself at the accreditation window and surrendered her bag and purse. She heard a nurse saying,

"And write, 'Happy Days to my friend, Eliza Decima!' "

The steel-tonsilled voice of the guard came through the speaker.

"What is *this*, nurse?" He had taken the wax-wrapped "dough nut" from her bag.

"It's — um — something my patient asked for. A sort of pastry."

The guard sniffed it. "No accounting for tastes," he snorted. "Colonel Jansen is still briefing the nurses, but I'm afraid you're in the soup, Tertia."

"The darned subway! I was lucky not to get a rail through my heart!"

"Is that a fact? My goodness."

The guard smirked as she recovered her bag and purse and hurried toward a locked door.

"That's it, ladies," she heard the ratter say, and she glanced at where Captain Tuggey was waiting.

"Guard, shall I go up with the young lady?" he said.

The guard nodded. The king of the ratters carried his cage to the door and winked at Eliza, who smiled back.

"A rat in *our* hospital?" she asked.

"Probably a hallucination. Very difficult breed to trap. We use poisoned gin as bait."

A battery of deadlocks chattered, and the door opened. Eliza started down a long doorless corridor leading to a distant gleam of stainless steel. The exterminator caught up in a few strides. Behind them the door closed with a dry, rattling musketry. Captain Tuggey looked back.

"No way out but up, eh?"

"The director is big on security."

Eliza stole a glance at the man's face. Her nurse's eye appraised his color, which was healthy, and noted the tiny fishbonelike white scars on his cheekbones and hands. He wore a ruffianly auburn mustache, and his face looked like that of a tough and resourceful man. Equal to anything.

He hummed as they walked. She was rather abashed by the big man. He must have great ability, courage, and a lot of money. He probably employed a half-million men and women who did daily battle with the vermin infesting the nation, exterminators who had the skill and courage to track, trick, and laserize the armies of ants, flotillas of mosquitoes, and legions of rats and mice who were about to inherit the earth now that all pesticides had been banned.

"Is that a cat or a terrier?" Eliza asked.

Tuggey held the cage so that she could see the face of a cat peering out. Its markings made it appear to be raffishly smiling.

"I do use terriers," he said, "but for a job like this I prefer cats. This one's a Kaffir cross. Want to hold him? He's gentle."

As the cat crawled into Eliza's arms, she exclaimed at his size and weight; he felt like nine kilograms of bone and sinew. When she squeezed a velvet paw, a set of long, glass-clear claws descended. The cat began to purr.

"Why, you're not fierce at all, kitty!" she murmured.

Tuggey chuckled. "Tell that to the rats!"

They reached the elevator door, where she used her identity card to summon the car.

"Where do you live, Eliza?"

"Harley Mansions — you know, out beyond Dome Four."

"Tough neighborhood. The rats don't all have four legs, either."

"I carry a stunner, of course. Stun a man, kill a rat."

"You should have a cat, child. I could loan you one."

She glanced at him, wondering if he were leading up to something. But he must know that nurse-clones did not date. Had he smelled her perfume and drawn a false conclusion?

"I'm afraid one cat couldn't deal with all the rats in the mansion," she said. "I bought one from a peddler once, for three hundred new Clarks. The rats killed him in forty-eight hours!"

"Never buy a cat from a peddler. That's an axiom. A cat like I'm thinking of would civilize your flat in a hurry."

How does he know I have a flat? she wondered. Most people were lucky to have a room.

"That would be nice," she said cautiously. "I — I'll let you know."

He shrugged. The elevator arrived and they rocketed upward, fifty-four floors nonstop.

3

In the small, cheerful lobby at the top, there was a fragrance of orange blossoms and a mumble of music. In one corner sat a very old couple with an overnight bag on the floor between them. Eliza smiled at them and fluttered her fingers.

"Are you taking us to Valhalla?" cried the old woman.

"No, dears," Eliza said, tapping her lips to remind them Valhalla was top secret. "A special nurse will come for you."

"Well, we've been waiting a half hour," the old man complained, "and it seems to me —"

A bell rang, and both old people, perfect examples of the superannuated Guppy, sat back and went silent. Eliza knew they had been warned to speak to no one after leaving the downstairs lobby.

In their probably two hundred years, they had evolved into something quite different from what they had been all those generations ago. The translucency of their faces, like clear jelly spread over their skulls, revealed a network of tendons and blood vessels. Yellowish eyes with pinpoint pupils peered out of concentric rings of muscle tissue; their mouths were purselike openings in a macramé of fine yellowish cords. These were the outward manifestations of Guppyism, only one of the disadvantages of living to a ripe old age — of never saying die.

"We won the trip to Valhalla in a Suicide Bingo parlor!" the old woman blurted.

"Shh! You aren't supposed to talk about it, dear."

Eliza glanced at the ratter. Fortunately, he was doing something with the cat, and seemed not to have heard any of this. She hurried to a reception window, where a black-wigged woman glared out at her.

"Well, Eliza Tertia?" the woman said.

"I'm sorry —! The subway —"

"Tell Colonel Jansen about it. She's still briefing the nurses."

"I — I'm sorry; ashamed —"

"And by the way, Zone Blue is off limits today. Committee of Thirteen meeting."

The ratter came into view, and the receptionist gasped. "Who is that?" she demanded.

"It's Captain Tuggey — the exterminator. Didn't they tell you he was riding up with me?"

"No. They did not." The woman stared bitterly at the nurse, then put on a smile for the famous exterminator.

"I hope you didn't hear any of our little secrets?"

"Secrets?" Tuggey shrugged. "No, ma'am. I'm here to catch a rat, and that's about the size of it."

The Committee of Thirteen was another family secret, and Eliza was pretty sure he must have heard the receptionist's brassy voice.

"Colonel Jansen is in the briefing room, Captain," said the receptionist. "She'll show you where the rat was seen. You can go with Eliza Tertia."

The door opened, and they started down a hall running out to the south face of the flat-topped pyramid.

"Come on, Eliza," the ratter teased. "What's the Committee of Thirteen?"

"I have no idea," she said primly.

He chuckled. "Everybody's heard about it. But what do they do?"

"Well — since it's leaked out anyway — it's a team of scientists working on Substance 1000 — and don't ask me what *that* is! The secret part is that they meet here, so please forget that you heard it. Here's the briefing room. You'll have to wait outside."

Eliza slipped into a room with a glowing green word board at the near end, and a dozen tall desks where eleven nurses identical to Eliza stood at attention. A slender, red-wigged woman in administrative green overalls stood at the board. She glanced coldly at Eliza, who ducked her head, murmured, and took her place behind the twelfth desk.

Colonel Jansen, the head nurse of all the hundreds of nurses in the hospital, resumed her briefing.

"— The other new patient is Rosalie Pollock. She's yours, Eliza Nona. Logardo's syndrome."

Fiercely she wrote the patient's name on the board

in incandescent white. Other names and medical data glowed there. Jansen was a tall woman with the shape of a dagger, and she impressed Eliza as being made out of some bloodless substance like canned salmon.

"That's all. Carry on," she said. "Eliza Tertia, stay."

The room drained like a bathtub, the nurses scurrying out in their blue duty coveralls. "Change," Jansen told Eliza. Eliza opened her locker and slipped out of her off-duty pinks and into her duty blues. Jansen talked.

"Absolutely inexcusable," she said. "Two days in a row!"

"I'm sorry. There was — the subway —"

"Oh, I realize you have an excuse! That's the way you play your stupid little game!"

Eliza gasped, pointing at the solid wall of monitors behind the head nurse. "Look! The subway accident . . ."

A squad of workmen around a battered subway car.

. . . THE SABOTEUR WAS A MALE JUVIE, ABOUT FORTY-THREE YEARS OLD, WHO RAN OFF SHOUTING, "BAN REJUVENAL NOW! ELEPHANT PLAN!" HE MADE HIS ESCAPE IN——

Jansen flicked off the set. "A sensible nurse allows for such delays, you know that. Starting tomorrow, you'll go on nights. And *what* have you done to your hair, by the way? Elizas are wearing curls this month, if you'll recall."

Eliza touched her hair self-consciously.

"Yes, Colonel, I know. But one day when my hair came unpinned, Evan said he liked —"

"Curls don't come unpinned, and do *not* use your patient's name! Great Galen! If Doctor Corday himself hadn't specified you for duty on this case —!"

Eliza choked, pointing at another of the monitors. "Head Nurse!" she said. "The ratter — Zone Blue —!"

Colonel Jansen whirled. One of the hallway monitors showed movement. In a dead-end corridor, Captain Tuggey was leaning against the elevator door in Zone Blue, watching two animals fight on the floor. Jansen pressed a button.

"Captain Tuggey. Freeze in place. Captain Tuggey! Come on!"

They left the briefing room at a trot, turned one way, then another, and together reached a stub of hallway boring into the inner core of service rooms. The walls, floor, and ceiling of this area were dark blue. The spur contained nothing but a locked elevator that Eliza knew went somewhere above. Beyond fifty-four there was only the roof garden — Valhalla — and the car did not go there. So where?

Casually, Captain Tuggey pulled on heavy ratter's gloves. Sam, the huge Kaffir cat, was finishing up a large brown rat, snarling as he worked. Tuggey gave Jansen a piratical wink.

"Sam and I don't fool around, lady. You're Jansen, eh?"

Jansen said tightly, "Yes, Captain, I am Colonel Jansen."

"Pleasure. Unfortunately, the rat is a nursing mother, so there has to be a nest nearby."

17

"Captain, did you not know that Zone Blue is off limits today, even to the nurses?"

Tuggey solemnly scratched his nose. "Ma'am, I invoke the Hot-Pursuit Law. Sam was right on the rat's tail."

Surreptitiously, Eliza glanced around. Her work had never taken her inside Zone Blue before. Near the elevator door, she saw a device like an old Roman coin, but the image on it was that of Evan's father, Dr. Walter Stevens Clark.

"Please bear in mind," said Jansen, "that you are here on sufferance. Deal with your cat and clean up the mess he's made."

"Righto," Tuggey said. "By the way, Colonel, where does the elevator go? Some special floor, eh?"

"The elevator is not your concern." Turning to Eliza, Jansen said caustically, "Since there's still a little time left today, why don't you get along to your patient, Eliza Tertia?"

van had been alone for nearly fifteen minutes when the door opened and Eliza Tertia came in. He knew her at once by the pleasant vanillalike scent she wore.

"Sorry I'm late," she said, as she got to work.

She looked at his chart, studied his meters, made entries in a ledger, then inspected a small black sphere, about the size of a handball, spinning on a pivot atop a small walnut box. There was an index number in a window, and she entered this figure on a chart. She seemed nervous.

Evan himself was trembling with anticipation. He felt fearful, yet happy, like the Friday night last fall when he had been sent in to play against a lineman who outweighed him by nearly forty pounds. His head told him he'd be demolished, his heart said, Charge!

Crazy with excitement, he made the first step.

"What's that thing, Eliza?" He pointed at the black ball.

"That? It's a holosphere. Please be quiet now."

"But what's it for?" Evan already had a theory.

She waved the stylus she was writing with. "Oh, Evan! You know I'm not supposed to answer questions. But all right. It's a thing that records everything that happens here, and feeds the picture to the guard, so he doesn't have to keep looking in."

"And what's the green button do?"

"Plays previous material backward — the re-spin."

When her back was turned, Evan reached out and touched the re-spin button. Now, if he understood her, the guard was watching the scene played backward, if indeed he was watching it at all. But since Eliza was not moving, how could he tell backward from forward? He watched the small window in the door, but the guard's face did not appear.

"Why can't you tell me anything, Eliza Tertia?" he asked.

"Because we don't want to contaminate your mind with new impressions."

"I've got the impression," said Evan, "that I'm thirsty."

His heart was pounding, but Eliza did not notice the meters racing. She brought him a glass of water and bent to prop him with one arm so that he could drink without spilling. He sipped, sank back with a sigh, and, moving his right hand to the wall, rapped the rim of the glass against it. It shattered, and he now held only the base and a jagged fragment. His hand shook uncontrollably as he stared at her.

"Eliza —" he croaked.

"Pshaw! Well, that's all right," Eliza said brightly.

Evan waited until she leaned over to collect the fragments, then placed the sharp point of the broken tumbler against her throat. She looked at him, puzzled first, then shocked. The clear, shining fang dimpled her flesh above a throbbing blood vessel.

"Evan —!" she gasped.

Shivering, Evan said, "D-don't m-move, Eliza! Or I'll slash you —" A cloud of stars shimmered about him; an arctic wind blew against his skin. The cold weakness was coming in again like a fog.

"Please don't, Evan," Eliza said. The pupils of her eyes were huge, and her lips remained parted. She wore the rapt expression of someone trying to thread a very fine needle.

"The recorder's running backward, so don't count on the guard," Evan said, his teeth chattering. The room was going dark. He could feel her breath against his cheek, warm and intimate.

"May I sit on the edge of your bed?" she whispered. "I can't hold this position long."

"All right. Keep your . . . back . . . to the door. . . ."

She let herself down on the edge of the mattress and waited. But at that instant, Evan's arm gave way, collapsing onto the mattress beside him. The nurse reached out and picked up the broken glass, without fuss. To his surprise, she did not call the guard.

"Evan, I'm *so* sorry!" she whispered. "I knew it was terrible for you, but I didn't know how terrible. I haven't worked on a re-an case before, you see."

His strength had leaked away like water; he could scarcely see her for the stars swirling between them.

"Brain . . . brain damage?" he said.

"No, no, nothing like that. You've been asleep. In cyronic suspension, you see. Frozen? You know. Or maybe you don't?"

He gripped the blanket with his fists, felt her fingers stroking his left hand. "Now, I'm going to turn up your heat, and you'll feel better right away," she said.

And in a few moments a warmth like a summer sun cocooned him. The nurse was still there when his head cleared, her rather large, sober mouth smiling as he looked at her. She seemed much too young for what was, presumably, a fairly responsible job. A few freckles on her nose enhanced her look of immaturity.

"I'm a better nurse than you think, Evan," she said. "If I haven't told you anything, it's because I have strict orders not to. But a good nurse knows when to break rules, as well as keep them. And if you'll promise not to tell anyone, I'll tell you as much as I can."

"Thanks," he said. "What's a re-an case?"

"Reanimation — brought back to life. They used to do it all the time. But you're the first to be brought out of cyronic suspension in quite a while. You've been in that state for — well, for some time, and now we're bringing you back!" She beamed.

Evan sank deeper into his pillowed warmth. A foghorn of alarm howled in him. "Somehow, Eliza," he said, "that isn't the great news you seem to think. Because where I live, they only freeze carrot and salamander cells."

An electric spark leaped in his head and he had

22

another vision. *Dr. Hawkins handing him a half-frozen lab animal. "Here's another mouse for your owl, Evan." Dr. Hawkins moving cylinders of gas into the elevator to take down into his silo-lab.*

"Not to worry," Eliza said cheerfully. "They made tremendous progress in cryonics after Hawkins' Principle was discovered. There were zillions of bodies in Lazarus Society vaults awaiting re-an. Well, still are! And they'll keep on waiting. But you're special!"

He tried to say something, but only snored, and she waited while he was siphoned back into a memory of that morning — riding off on his moped on August 12, 1984, the year made famous by George Orwell. But not so bad, after all. A lovely day for Humboldt County, in fact, on the foggy northern California coast. He had ridden out into the woods to the old missile silo where Hawkins lived in a homemade Lincoln-Log sort of cabin. Evan mowed the grass for him, sawed wood, and did other chores. But this morning the scientist wasn't around, and the grass needed cutting, so —

". . . founded the Lazarus Society," Eliza Tertia was reciting. "He got millions of names on petitions, and they made it legal for human beings to be stored — sick people, you see, awaiting cures for their particular illnesses —"

Nineteen eighty-four . . . And what year was it now? Afraid to ask, he nibbled at it.

"But I wasn't sick. Where did they find me? And how did I get here?"

"Well, sweetie," Eliza said with a sigh, "you were found by rangers in the Northern California Oxygen

Wilderness two weeks ago, in an old missile silo. There was another body there, an old man, but he died as — well, never mind that."

"And they brought me here?"

"They brought you here."

"Where is 'here'?"

"Los Angeles, the nation's capital."

"You're losing me," Evan muttered. "Washington, D.C. is — okay, so Hawkins pulled a fast one on me. Froze me! Wait'll I catch up with that clown —!"

"Oh, he's dead, long since. It's" — Eliza smiled sadly — "later than you may think, Evan. Two thousand one hundred sixty-four, in fact. You were asleep for one hundred and eighty years, apparently."

There were tears behind Evan's eyes, tears as cold and heavy as drops of mercury. But by strength of will he held them, staring at the ceiling. Then he turned his head and looked out the window. All he could see were spires — spiky ones, under what looked like the lofty glass roof of a botanic garden. All this information Eliza had been feeding him was like foreign coins: curious and strange, of a certain value; but how much?

Was it all a very involved farce? Still a hallucination? He peered around for pranksters, or one-way mirrors. Suddenly an idea stirred in the cold mire of his mind: A test!

"What's the name of my father's pet rat?" he asked.

"Methuselah!" she said, proudly.

He squinted then, trying to get a handle on what he was proving. Aha! "You're in on it, all right," he said.

24

"In on what?"

"The joke. How would anyone in 2164 know about my father's rat?"

She raised her hands and let them drop in her lap. "But that's what it's all about, sweetie!" she said. "Longevity! Methuselah the rat was given shots of a drug your father discovered called Rejuvenal, and he lived to be twenty-three years old. And people have been getting Rejuvenal after a certain age for — oh, for a *long* time. Evan, I studied about your family in American history, and in medical school I learned all about Methuselah. We used to tell each other shivery stories about what happened to Evan Clark, like the princes who were murdered in the Tower! And then, two weeks ago, we learned that for some reason Doctor Hawkins had put you into cryonic suspension."

Evan knew he was going to throw up, or scream, or hurl himself out the window. Because something in his head told him it was all true, not a hallucination.

It was indeed later than he had thought.

"I'm going to sleep awhile," he whispered.

"Do. And don't worry. Eliza won't let anything happen to you."

He said, with a hard stare, but in a croak, "I don't need anybody's help, Eliza. I can handle it."

"Of course you can."

"And get this straight," he said, "I want my clothes. I'm leaving here when I wake up. And when I do, all hell's going to break loose."

He sank into a sleep like a cold, dark lake.

5

Depressed, Eliza emerged from the hospital onto the deserted walk. Seventeen hundred. The fortified air under the dome was hot and oppressive. Most Dome Seven Guppies were off the street in air-conditioned apartments. The parking strip across from the hospital was dotted with magnasliders—doctors' vehicles, administrators', rich Guppy patients'.

Eliza had just come from a humiliating dressing-down by Head Nurse Jansen, who had let her wait forty minutes before the interview. "Dragon!" she whispered, turning toward the subway. Then she heard a drone of electric motors and a swish of air. A small green van-type slider floated out into the street from the parking area. On its side she saw the pouncing-cat emblem of Captain Tuggey's exterminating firm. With Tuggey grinning roguishly at the tiller, the van pulled up beside her and sank to earth as he lessened the force that enabled it to float above the iron particles in the street.

"Get in!" he called. "Where to?"

Eliza hesitated, frowning. He was responsible for at least some of her problems today, since he had certainly done nothing to improve Colonel Jansen's state of mind. But the prospect of a cool ride tempted her. So she shrugged, for his benefit, and got in, placing her bag at her feet and her purse on her lap. The air of the cab was deliciously cool and aromatic. Tuggey twisted the handle of the tiller and the motors sang. The little van rushed forward, rocking on its cushion of magnetic force.

"Late again!" he said. "My, oh my, Eliza."

"You're not so early yourself," sniffed Eliza. "Considering that you found your rat hours ago."

"But not the nest. How did the chat go with the Ice Queen? I heard her call you to her office, didn't I?"

"Probably. You seem to see all and hear all."

"What happened?"

"I go on dogwatch tomorrow night. Sixteen hundred to twenty-four hundred. Plague take her!"

"Just because you were late?"

"Not *just* because. Partly because she was mad at you. Stop here," she said curtly. "I'll miss my train if we gab all evening."

Tuggey laughed. "Sweetheart, you won't miss anything. I'll give you a ride home. You are in a state, aren't you?"

Eliza raised her hand to protest, but he cruised right past the subway hole. Actually, she was too

27

tired and nervous to refuse the offer of a ride, and even if she broke another rule by accepting it, Jansen couldn't take her off the case, because she was Dr. Corday's personal choice.

"Or better still," said Tuggey, "why not have dinner at my place? I've just talked with my cook, and it's ocean fish tonight, and maybe some fruit. What do you say?"

"No, I really — No, Captain —"

"Wonderful woman, my cook. She's called Mom, and my head security man is called Pop, a retired police chief. Sweet old couple."

"Actually, Captain, the rule —"

"I live in a little backwater we call Piccadilly. Almost like Old England. Need to shop? Everything you need, within reason. Stuff you can't even find in Dome Seven. Illegal weapons, black-market food, cut-rate oxygen —"

Eliza giggled and relaxed. Why argue? He was obviously used to getting his own way, and there was no good reason why she should not enjoy a good meal for a change.

"What's a rich man doing in a place like Piccadilly?" she asked.

"I like to be near my animals. And the Guppies — woops, Seniors — would go up the wall if I raised cats and dogs in one of the domes."

Fifteen minutes later they passed through the air lock and left the dome. Other domes rose lumpily here and there on the drab skyline of the great city, like beehives. They *were* hives, Eliza reflected — hives for ancient drones, unproductive, waspish, and voracious. They produced nothing, devoured all.

Outside the domes sprawled thousands of acres of ancient buildings, some tall, many of only three or four stories. These were the type of neighborhoods known as dead city areas.

They were far from devoid of life, however, only of certain utilities. People swarmed in them, in an economy like that of the ocean floor, the denizens feeding upon and being devoured by each other. There was little they could afford to buy in the domes, but little they needed, either. The young people who lived here — sixty years and under — made up only thirty percent of the population, which was glutted with superannuated citizens. By means legal and otherwise, they traded, bartered, stole, and manufactured what they needed.

The heat grew less oppressive, and greenery began to sprout — tufts of grass, trees, fenced and guarded vegetable patches. The polluted air was so rich in carbon dioxide that green things prospered, collecting carbon dioxide and paying a modest dividend of oxygen.

The street life, too, grew richer. Tuggey piloted the van through lines of open-air stalls, barrows, sidewalk gin shops, and repairmen's crannies. He parked.

"Let's do your shopping first," he said. "They'll close and disappear soon."

A half-dozen young men hurried up. "Watch your slider, mister?" they yelled, jostling each other.

Tuggey chose a tall boy with a shaven skull and a head decal, like most of the young fellows, and tossed him a coin. "Ten Clarks now, ten when we get back."

Eliza got out a list of items she hoped to find, and

Tuggey moved through the crowd like an icebreaker. A barber with a chair on the sidewalk clinked his shears at him. "Trim that mustache, sir?"

Tuggey grinned. "Sure — someday," he said.

They passed a cart where a young woman in overalls was selling little bottles of colored water decorated with twisted wire, in a pathetic attempt at folk art. Eliza bought a green cough syrup vial adorned with aluminum wire. The vendor pressed a purple flask on the ratter.

"And you, sir?"

"Someday." He smiled, and flipped her a coin. They moved on, buying a banana, some fine beefsteak tomatoes, a small loaf of dark bread. Eliza saw a barrow of green metal bottles, and said quickly:

"Oh, and I need oxygen! But, pshaw, I don't have a trade-in, so . . ."

Tuggey said to the oxygen vendor, "Let's have two of those."

The vendor was a red-faced man of middle age with upturned black brows that made him look satanic. "Just like that, eh, mate? No trade-in?"

"Oh, well, someday," Tuggey said casually. And Eliza looked at him curiously. *Someday*: It was an odd little catchword he used, and in this case it snapped the man to attention.

"Oh, sorry, Captain — didn't recognize you. Two, nurse? No hurry on the trade-ins."

They returned to the van, and the ratter headed the slider down the alley. Suddenly there was a brick wall before them which became a door, and they crossed a small cobbled courtyard, and another door opened in another wall. They glided into a large, well-lit room, like a small warehouse, and the van sank to the floor. Around the walls were banks of cages. Eliza perked up, hearing cats. An old man in black work clothes was filling feed trays. He stared at them. Though he must have been at least eighty, he was tall and well-fleshed.

"How's she going, Pop?" said Tuggey.

"You should have signaled that you were coming in, Bill," the old man complained. "I am the chief custodian of these premises. Now, if you don't feel you need me —"

Tuggey grinned. "Sorry, Pop! This is Eliza Tertia — don't know your last name, nurse."

"Gamble." Eliza offered her hand.

"Hello, Gamble," grumbled the old man.

"Pick out a cat for Nurse Gamble," said Tuggey. "A loner, but not an old tom on crutches."

"Well — Attila would fill the bill, I guess, although he's got a torn claw. . . ."

"I can treat it!" Eliza exclaimed. "Oh, he sounds fierce!"

"I'll bring him in at dinner time. Excuse me, Gamble, I've got to finish with these cats."

6

*T*hey went through a tiny vestibule, where Eliza knew they were being scrutinized; then she found herself in the alcoved end of a very long living room. The room was huge and grand, with dove gray carpeting and antique furniture, much of it apparently genuine twentieth century. One long wall was absolutely plain, and Tuggey said, indicating a button in the near wall:

"Press it."

She did, and caught her breath. The wall melted away and revealed a Japanese garden, with a stone temple, raked gravel paths, small twisted pines, and a pond lapping the very edge of the carpet. Though she knew it was merely an holistic illusion, a picture in 3-D, she could actually hear wind chimes and smell the pines.

A door opened and a small elderly woman came from a kitchen, wearing a dress and apron. Eliza remembered pictures in history books of the early days in the West. The captain introduced them, and the old lady came forward, pecked Eliza on the cheek, and welcomed her.

"Well, lands, I promised Bill fresh fish," she said, "but all I've got is wieners. How about a picnic on the beach? Hot dogs, potato salad, and pink lemonade!"

"Fine," Tuggey said. "You'll want to freshen up, Eliza. Show her the way, Mom."

So Eliza got a peek at a bedroom almost the size of the parlor, a bathroom meters across, and everything antique and sumptuous. For all his down-to-earth airs, the ratter was obviously an extremely wealthy man. When she returned, the Japanese garden had vanished and the wall was now a seashore, where peaceful sunset waves dissolved into lace on the sand. Before this illusion of a beach a tablecloth had been spread, and there were low canvas seats. Mom was setting out paper plates and the air was spicy with the fragrances of wieners and pickle relish.

Eliza took one of the seats, and Pop deposited in her lap a gigantic Siamese cat with a creamy body and chocolate points. She crooned as she stroked him, and felt the scar tissue of a hundred memorable rat fights under his short fur. He wore a collar with silver studs.

"Pop, he's wonderful!" She broke off as she saw that a young man in a black jump suit had joined them. His features were Indian, and he gazed at her in suspicion.

"This is that Guppy nurse, eh?" he muttered.

"This is Eliza Gamble," said the exterminator. "And this is Indio, Eliza, one of my night men."

Eliza said hello. Pop said, "How many tons of sparklers did you put into orbit for humanity today?"

"Plenty, old man," Indio said.

"Indio's a worker at a space-scow port," said Tuggey. "The administration hasn't made much of it yet, but recently we've been disposing of two hundred years of nuclear waste by launching it into space."

"But I thought it was against international law!" Eliza exclaimed.

"It is. That's why they're playing it down."

"What bothers me," Indio said glumly, "is what if somebody out there turns it around and fires it back?"

When everyone was seated, Mom passed around glasses of pink lemonade. Pop raised his. "Bottoms up!" he said. "Used to say that when I was a kid."

Eliza sipped at the drink, finding it so tasty that she downed it in a few gulps. "Delicious!"

Mom was right there to refill the glass for her.

"Thank you. I've never tasted anything so good."

"It's the maraschino cherry flavor. Well, goodness, you wouldn't know about that, poor dear. Makes it pink and gives it spice."

It — or something else in the drink — also caused a tiny spot of warmth to glow like a pilot light under Eliza's wishbone. She felt as though she were going up in a balloon. They passed around a tray of wieners in something called "buns," a soft bread she had never tasted before. As they ate, the sun sank into slate blue waves, and Eliza smelled seaweed and brine and felt a breeze on her face. The illusion was complete.

Yet suddenly the melancholy time of day, the chilling of the air and death of the sun, began to affect her deeply. To her surprise, tears came to her eyes. Into her mind there crowded her worries over Evan Clark and her clashes with Colonel Jansen. She thought hopelessly of her wretched little flat, and the racket from the gin mill downstairs.

"What's wrong, dearie?" Mom asked gently. "You're crying."

"It's nothing. . . ."

"Now, you aren't on duty here. You can let your hair down — that's a saying we used to have," Mom added.

Eliza was afraid to confide in them, knowing that once she started she might wind up screaming her hatred for President Fallon, Dragon Jansen, and Dr. Corday. Then she thought, in confusion, But I *don't* hate them, I *love* them! I just hate the way things are.

She was too confused to know what she thought.

"It's just I'm worried over so many things," she said. "And as far as I can tell, everything is going to get worse — the shortages, old people gobbling up all the necessities and living longer and longer. . . . I'm sorry, Mom and Pop, I didn't mean you."

Tears were flowing down her cheeks, and she had to bite her lip to choke back her sobs! What was wrong with her?

"It's been a hard day, hasn't it, dear?" soothed Mom.

"Terrible. Just terrible."

Bill Tuggey sat by her and put a thimble-sized glass in her hand.

"Help settle you down," he murmured. "Cordial." It looked like cough syrup. The Code did not permit her to drink anything alcoholic, but the drink looked harmless enough, and perhaps it would take the edge off this dreadful depression that had its fangs at her throat. She sipped it, murmured, and took the rest in a gulp.

That was the last clear thought she had.

Someone was saying, "I'm terrified about what they're going to do to him! He's such a nice boy. And I've always loved the stories about him — I studied his life story in medical school, did my thesis on his last day in Ferndale. And now Superpsych — Doctor Corday, the hospital head — is getting ready for brain scans! I don't trust him! I think he's vicious! He might — I don't know. . . ."

It took her a moment to realize it was her own voice rattling on this way, and she knew she was about to tell everything she had stifled so long. . . .

7

The sun drowned in the salty sea, night rolled up from the horizon, and the room itself grew dark. A small crackling campfire had materialized before Eliza. Off to one side she saw a little sign, placed askew in the sand: CENTERVILLE BEACH. Centerville! Why, that was the beach where Evan and his friends used to come, nearly two hundred years ago! She felt the rumble of the big cat purring in her lap.

People were drifting down the beach and taking places on the sand — the carpet, that is. Did she recognize some of them? A man in a barber's jacket; a tall youth whom Indio called Corky; a young woman in work overalls; a red-faced, middle-aged man with satanic eyebrows. Where had she seen them before?

"Someday," Captain Tuggey had said to each of them. And now here they were at the beach party.

"You might as well get it off your chest," the ratter said, "before it goes sour. What happened?"

"My patient threatened to kill me!"

Tuggey glanced at the big red-faced man, who looked grave. "Buzz, this sounds like your department." The man moved to sit near Eliza. "This is Doctor Lionel Baker, Eliza. We call him Buzz. He's a neurosurgeon, used to practice at Clark Memorial —"

"Doctor Lionel Baker?" Eliza gasped. "Why, there's a plaque on the neuro floor —"

"Long time ago," said Dr. Baker. "Doctor Corday and I didn't hit it off, and my license was lifted. I'm selling oxygen now. Job with a lot of pressure." The blue eyes in the rosy face was puckish. "What's Corday told Evan about his situation?"

"Nothing!" Eliza wailed. "He thinks he's got a tumor or something. He's terrified. Today he broke a water glass, put the edge to my throat, and made me tell him everything I knew."

Baker snorted. "Corday is a butcher. Evan should have been getting bits of the story as soon as he was able to understand. Why haven't they been prepping him?"

Eliza hesitated; but she had lost the famous reticence of the Eliza clones, and she blurted out: "Doctor Corday says we mustn't contaminate his mind with new impressions. When we start the brain scans, he wants the facts to be as fresh as possible."

"You're talking about Substance 1000?"

"Yes. They want to get the formula out of his brain, so that people can live — well, forever! And no young person will ever be able to get a job, or live in anything but a kennel, and —"

"What they want, then," said Dr. Baker, "is his memory. Corday regards the rest as waste. What have they told you nurses about Evan's last days?"

"Nothing we didn't already know from medical school. About his father's discovering Rejuvenal. And that before it had been released for use, he developed a new drug that he called Substance 1000, which wouldn't have that awful Guppy side effect, and might make us practically immortal. The day he dictated the elements of the discovery to a thing they called a 'tape recorder,' Evan was working in his father's lab, feeding dead mice to his burrowing owl. He was very interested in natural history!" she said with animation. "He spent days and days camping in the woods, learning about — oh, and he made a model of how a rattlesnake injects venom —"

Buzz patted her hand. She *was* apt to go on when she got on the subject of Evan, she knew. She had an Evan scrapbook — pictures of him, of his home, even a letter he'd written to his girlfriend, Sherrill Dobson. What a price she'd paid the antiquarian for *that!*

"Yes, I know," said Buzz Baker. "But you were telling us about their ransacking his mind for the formula."

Her mind was wandering. The pink lemonade and the cordial had affected her. "Well, I think Doctor Clark was having second thoughts about extending the life span. He felt that there was a right time to die, as well as to be born. How many years of being useful and creative and happy, as far as that goes? Want to know what I think?"

She looked around at the group on the sand. There must be fifty of them now, very determined-looking people, from eigtheen to eighty, she guessed, listening intently.

"*I* think Doctor Clark deliberately erased the tape, and when government scientists asked him later for the formula, he just *pretended* to forget! Corday and Jansen would *kill* me for saying that! The search for longevity is holy writ around Clark Memorial."

"So to sum it up," said Buzz Baker, "the facts are there in Evan's brain, because he heard his father dictate them. And by proper stimulation of the neural cells, they can be recovered — he'll rattle them off like a ventriloquist's dummy. And then they can turn the new stuff loose on our sad and tattered country."

Eliza nodded. "And the reason they're so big on security," she said rashly, "is that they're afraid somebody else will get at Evan, and kill him to destroy the formula!"

There was an awkward silence. The big ratter stood beside her.

"Yes, there are plenty of people who would do that," he agreed. "But the responsible ones merely want to get hold of the boy and etch those few minutes from his mind. It's very simple, and safe, with low-power laser-fogging. The brain is Buzz's field, you see. And we plan to do it, once we get him."

"And you want me to help you get him," Eliza murmured drowsily. "You're all Juvies! This is a Juvenile Underground cell!"

"Yes, dear," Mom said. "There are people as old as Methuselah in the underground. People who are sick of living at the expense of young people who are being stifled. We think the suicide epidemic is shameful — and that Logardo's syndrome! Now,

40

shouldn't there be a more dignified way to go than that?"

"The Elephant Plan," Eliza murmured. "I see the graffiti everywhere —"

"Well, we don't have the details ironed out yet," said Tuggey, "but we're definitely into it. One thing at a time, though. Right now we have a crisis. We have to get Evan out of that mausoleum. Do you think he'd cooperate?"

"Of course! He's planning to escape, anyway. But there's really no way you can do it."

"What's upstairs — the Valhalla thing?"

"It's a lovely suicide garden — visitors know they're going to die, only they don't know exactly when. People play Suicide Bingo — it's the only form of suicide President Fallon has approved — and if they win, they go to Valhalla for a few days. And some night they don't wake up. I was up there once with Jansen when someone needed care. It's beautiful — an artificial rain forest, and all the natural things they used to love, but can't have anymore because nature is off limits in this country. Like the redwoods where Evan lived . . ."

"How many guards?"

"None. Just a few attendants."

"Tell us about the Committee of Thirteen," Tuggey said.

She was being pumped outrageously, she knew. She didn't care. "All I know is that they're outstanding scientists, and they meet once a week in Zone Blue."

"Tomorrow night you and I are going up to the Committee's conference room."

41

"No. No, really! Jansen might be watching the monitors."

"I'll take care of Jansen. I want to see what's up there. Maybe some key to getting Evan out. Doesn't it strike you as odd that they work right in the hospital, but you've never seen them?"

"No. It's all so secret."

"I've set it up with Jansen for me to work tomorrow night," the ratter said. "A cock-and-bull story about nocturnal rats, so I need to work after dark. You're on nights now, Eliza. You'll forget most of what we've said here tonight, but you'll leave Evan for a break at exactly twenty-two hundred tomorrow night, and you'll meet me in Zone Blue."

"But why me?"

"Because I may need you for cover."

She must have nodded off. When she opened her eyes, she was lying on a sofa, and there was a cup of coffee beside her. The cat was asleep in the hollow of her arm. The people had left. People? Had there really been people, or had she dreamed them?

"You dropped off, lovey," Mom said softly.

Eliza tried to remember. There had been a beach party — hadn't there? And yet —

"Drink your coffee," said Tuggey, stretching. "I'll run you over to Harley Mansions."

In the little van, they floated through dark streets where people slept on walks and in alleys. In a few minutes they were parking before one of the ancient ruins called Harley Mansions. Tall royal palms lined the street. On the ground floor was a gin mill — closed now, so it must be after two — and down the block was the reeking community garbage dump.

Refuse — at least what the rats hadn't eaten — was picked up at irregular intervals.

"Good night, Eliza."

"Good night."

From her purse she took her stunner, a small laser weapon capable of stunning hoodlums and killing rats, and climbed two floors to her flat. The cat sniffed along the splintered baseboards. She took out her keys and dealt with the array of locks on her door. There were seven — magic number guaranteeing safety. Inside, she locked up and tired to remember all the things that had happened. But the memory had almost completely faded. She had the impression of Captain Tuggey as a very important, powerful, and possibly dangerous man. And she recalled that she could sleep late, because she was on nights now. She wondered what Evan would think when a different clone came with his breakfast? Would she miss her?

The cat snuggled down by her pillow. "Good night, Attila!" she murmured.

"Good night, Eliza," he whispered back.

She rose on one elbow, shocked.

"It's me — Bill Tuggey," a voice from the cat's collar said. "If there's ever anything you want, just tell Attila. He'll be monitored at all times. Anything at all . . ."

She lay back, laughing softly. And fell asleep.

8

*E*van slept little that night, and at dawn, while Eliza Duodecima, his night nurse, was out of the room, he rose and stood looking down at the flat-roofed buildings and stubby towers below, trying to sort things out in his mind. At last he had a handle on his situation, a name for his problem:

Suspended animation.

All he had to do now was to account for the one hundred eighty years he had lost, and construct a reality he could live with. Problem solving, Dad called it. Or used to call it. Were his parents alive? Had they been preserved by that drug his father had been so proud of, to a ripe old two hundred twenty years or so? He was afraid they were still alive; afraid also that they were dead.

The great dome above this part of the city was turning pink. Today, he thought, is the first day of the rest of my life. A rather vapid saying that had a special meaning for him now. There had to be a lot of changes — unbelievable ones, the sheer weight of which might drive a person mad. Think of the changes in the years between 1800 and 1984: from horses, candlelight, and wooden dentures to jets, electricity, nuclear technology, and electronics.

It might be almost as bad in his own one-hundred-eighty-year gap.

I'd like to get it a little bit at a time, he thought, and I'd like to have it from someone I like and trust, like that little nurse. The other nurses were robots, Iron Eyes was a goosefleshy horror; but Eliza Tertia was genuine. She had called him sweetie yesterday, and had expressed sympathy. She was real.

He heard latches clicking, breakfast trolleys rattling along the corridor. A thought entered his mind like a mouse sniffing warily: If the folks were alive, they'd have come to see me.

Eliza Duodecima returned, made some entries in a ledger, and gave him a brief smile. " 'Bye, Evan. See you tomorrow."

The time plaque over the door said 0801. Eliza would be late of course; he liked that; showed she was human. But to his surprise she came in at 0802, right on schedule. His spirits bounded. He looked at her, grinning, anxious for contact. "Hi, Eliza!"

She came to his bedside, no smile or warmth, and studied his meters, smiling emptily. "Morning, Evan. How are you."

Not a question, just a blank statement. What's the weather like. Who's on first. There was a wisp of antiseptic about her, a crispness in her movements. No perfume! Rearing up, he stared at her.

45

"You aren't Eliza! Where is she?"

"Of course I'm Eliza. Eliza Septima —"

"I want Tertia! Get her!" His heart raced; there was a ringing in his ears. His panic shocked him. He realized she was his main hope to preserve his sanity, that he was really counting on her.

She put her hands on her hips in mock dismay. "Really! Aren't I good enough for you?"

A firecracker went off in his head. All at once he was shouting at her. At the core of his anger was the fear and hurt that Eliza had, after all, told on him, and gone off the case. A fink! He dragged the covers back and crawled out of bed, as the nurse pressed a button and the guard rushed in. He was yelling at them to get Eliza, get Eliza! His muscles were coming to life again, and the burly old guard had to lie on him to subdue him.

Soon the tall red-wigged woman in the special green coveralls, Jansen, appeared with a young doctor. They stood beside him, watching him struggle with the guard. Jansen said something to the doctor.

"Think not," the doctor said. "I don't understand this. Evan, what's the trouble?"

He cursed them.

Jansen got around behind the head of the bed and applied her fingertips to some pressure points in his neck, and he was instantly subdued. "Now, stop this, Evan. Tell us what you want."

"I want Eliza Tertia!"

"But they're all the same!" He could see her green eyes, dazzled with alarm, and knew she was probably responsible for him, and somebody would have her neck if he had a setback.

"Oh, no," he panted. "Oh, no! The rest are wind-ups. She's real. I want to talk to her."

"All right, Evan, let me explain. She's working nights now. She'll be here at sixteen hundred. Will you be quiet while I talk it over with the doctor?"

Sensing that he had leverage, he nodded; also the pain she was exerting in his neck was considerable. Colonel Jansen and the doctor huddled. Then the doctor raised his eyes.

"Eliza asked for the day off, young fellow," he said. "But if you want her, we'll get her. How's that?"

"Okay. Eliza Tertia, right? Nobody else."

Jansen said coldly to the doctor, "I'll ask Doctor Corday about a workup on Tertia. Maybe she's taking some drug. She's a clone, and she'd better remember it."

"Here's his breakfast!" cried Nurse Eliza Septima, relieved.

Everyone marveled and cooed, as though it were the news of the century. Clearly, they were anxious to get him back on the track. He was of great importance to them.

Ah-ha.

9

*E*liza arrived a couple of hours later. She was less neatly gotten-up than usual, and wore a cheap gray jump suit and a sort of lace doily over her hair, which apparently she had not had time to brush.

"Why, Evan! I'm surprised at you, she said as the other Eliza departed in a huff.

"A lot of people are going to be surprised at me," he said. "I'm going to rattle some chains. I'm getting out of here."

"Tut-tut," said Eliza, setting about her work.

"Why am I so important to Iron Eyes and Corday?" he asked.

"I can't answer that, Evan. You know the policy on talking."

"Have I ever had any visitors? What about my parents?"

"A woman called. She may be allowed to visit."

"Iron Eyes' wife?"

"Her name is Sherrill Leffler."

He squinted at her. "My girlfriend's name is Sherrill, but her last name is Dobson. Wait a minute! She must have married Rusty Leffler. But she'd be — good night! — nearly two hundred!"

"She said she's a friend of yours. By the way! You're going to have some visitors tonight. President Fallon and Doctor Corday."

"Iron Eyes is Fallon?"

Eliza shook her head. "Don't call him that, Evan. It's cruel. A deranged Juvie threw acid in his face years ago, and Doctor Corday built the receptor orbs for him. They want to talk to you and review your case."

"My case," Evan said thoughtfully. Swinging his legs over the edge of the bed, he sat there; saw the guard glance in. "What about Sherrill's case? If she's nearly two hundred, this Rejuvenal stuff must really work."

He got down on the floor and began doing push-ups.

"It has certain side effects — Guppyism, and some others."

He glanced up at her. "What about that other stuff Dad was working on? Substance 1000, he called it."

Eliza grimaced. "Don't tell me about it! Don't even think about it."

She looked terrified. He sat on the edge of the bed and studied her. "Why not? It was just another experimental —"

"Shhh!"

"Okay, okay. Does Sherrill still live in Ferndale? Or is it there, even?"

"No, she lives here in Dome Seven." She brightened. "But Ferndale's hardly changed! It was declared a national monument a century ago, and that whole part of Northern California is an Oxygen Wilderness. Off limits to nearly everyone."

"Why?"

"Because the wilderness generates oxygen. One of our nurses won a place on a guided tour through the redwoods last year! She saw birds, and a red fox, and — oh, a frog, a snake. . . ."

Evan began to get the gloomy picture of a world oversupplied with superannuated people but running short of everything else. "What's the birth rate?" he asked.

Rather, um, low. It's confidential, so I don't really know. But seventy percent of the population is over a hundred now, so —"

"Then why don't they ban Rejuvenal?"

"It *is* banned — except in the United States. You see, Charlie Fallon's Seniors party controls all the lawmaking, so it's hard to — well, effect any changes. The ban idea shows up on the ballot now and then, but Charlie's block — he prefers to be called Charlie — always votes it down."

Suddenly a bell began to ring, and Eliza came to attention. "Freeze in place!" she hissed.

He looked for the bell but could not find it. "What for?"

"Face the door and freeze!"

The guard opened the door and Jansen entered, flushed and excited. She made gestures toward Evan. "Please lie on your bed!"

Evan let himself be propped up. A sturdy old Guppy in a black work smock drove a small electric truck into the room. The cargo on its noseplate was compact but heavy, judging by the way the hard rubber wheels rumbled on the floor. The driver parked near the far wall, stepped down, and began stacking small metal ingots against it.

Evan studied them. They were gold in color, incised with numbers and symbols, and he was reminded of the ingots in Fort Knox, where the nation's gold supply was stored.

"What *are* those?" he asked.

"Gold," Jansen said. "Do be quiet, now."

As the first man left, another ancient workman drove a truck in and began stacking more gold bars. When he finished and wheeled smartly out, another man drove in.

"What is this?" Evan demanded. "*Romper Room?*" They ignored him. When the parade of electric trucks ended, a gold pyramid loomed against the wall, several feet wide at the base and four or five feet high. Then there were voices and footfalls, and the guard could be heard saying:

"Yes, *sir*, Mr. President! Pleased to see you, *sir!*"

"Hello, Brumitt," a man said, in a rather piping voice; and Iron Eyes walked in.

10

*H*e was a large man with thick white hair, a translucency in his skin, and a lantern jaw. It was Iron Eyes, all right, who had peered in at him so often while he was still in a partial coma. The man's orbs fascinated Evan. They were black crystal spheres with hundreds of facets, and they turned, in their metal sockets, with the faintest clicking.

The president extended his arms, beaming at Evan. He wore something like a gold jump suit.

"Welcome to the twenty-second century, my boy!" he cried.

Evan could think of nothing to say, so he muttered, "Hi."

The man dropped his head back and laughed, then turned and said to another man in the doorway, "He says, 'Hi!' Rodriguez! Just 'Hi.' Oh, that's rich! Put that down. For the media."

The second man was diminutive and frail, and reminded Evan of an old jockey, small-boned and with long iron gray hair and saturnine features. He wore a garment similar to that of Iron Eyes, but black with red shoulder boards. He wrote something in a notebook.

"Are you Charlie Fallon?" Evan asked.

"Yes, Evan. And I'm glad you didn't say 'President Fallon.' Because I'm Charlie to my friends, and you and I are going to be the best of friends. And this is General Rodriguez, who has charge of your safety here."

Rodriguez looked at Evan and grinned mirthlessly, like a monkey. His eyes were large, dark, and pessimistic.

Fallon raised one arm and beckoned. "Corday — come in here! Your personal physician, Evan, Doctor Thomas Corday, who has brought you along so ably from the twentieth century to the twenty-second!"

The doctor came in from the hall, a smiling, well-built man with reddish hair, a short beard, and greenish eyes. His face was translucent, and his flesh looked like ice-clear gelatin spread over a skull, with all the tendons and blood vessels intact. He wore a powder blue uniform.

"How are you today, Evan?" he asked.

Evan shrugged.

"Well!" The president strode to the pile of gold. "I'm sure you've been wondering about this," he said.

The more Evan heard, the less he liked what was going on, and the less he trusted any of these people. Fallon was obviously the one who had ordered him kept in the dark, and he was now about to wind him up like a toy to walk and talk a little.

"I decided it was my allowance, for mowing Hawkins' lawn," Evan added, pointedly.

"That rascal!" chuckled the president. "Yet in a way you're in his debt. If he hadn't stored you, we'd never have been able to meet like this, would we?"

Everyone except Eliza beamed at Evan. Their inability to understand what had happened to him was appalling. "Something else I owe him," he said, "is a crowbar over the head for killing my family."

"Oh, but, Evan! He didn't kill anybody. He —"

"Then where are they? Where are all my friends? Where's the world I lived in two weeks ago?"

Fallon's black-and-silver receptor orbs made a slight rasping as he swiveled them from one fact to another. He seemed not to comprehend. "But, my boy! You're in a better world now! And you're a *very* wealthy young fellow. All this gold is yours. This and much more!"

Evan turned aside. He could not regard the revolting capillary and tendon mask for long without getting queasy, especially when the president was bubbling with excitement, and spittle had formed in the corners of his mouth.

"I'm not getting this," he muttered. "What about the gold?"

"Your parents left a considerable sum in trust for you when they died, and of course the royalties from Rejuvenal have continued to pile up!"

Evan closed his eyes. It came as no surprise, now that he finally knew his parents were dead. He would experience grief later, but this morning he was too numbed by all that had happened, and was happening, to feel anything very keenly. It was one more shock to try to deal with.

"Nurse Gamble, let's have some light on the display!" Charlie Fallon cried.

Evan watched Eliza pick up a cordless lamp and tilt it. An intense white beam shot across the room. Her aim was bad: The bolt went straight into the leader's receptor orbs. He groaned and turned away, and Dr. Corday snapped:

"Clumsy little clone! For heaven's sake, Gamble —"

Eliza looked terrified. "I'm sorry! So clumsy of me!"

Fallon rubbed his brow. "Not her fault, Corday. Orbs have been needing adjustment. You can come to Lake House someday soon and do the work. You see, Evan," he went on, "your fortune is reckoned in the tens of billons of Clarks. You called them 'dollars,' but when they were revalued after their unfortunate decline, we put your father's portrait on the new bills, and people call them Clarks."

Evan shrugged. Everyone seemed to think that money could make up for losing your world and waking up in the deep freeze. He was supposed to be cheerful, whereas he was dazed with loss. Everyone was beaming at him, except Eliza, who looked miserable.

"Okay," Evan said, "I'm rich. What can I buy?"

"What," asked the ugly little genera, "do you want?"

"I want to go back to Ferndale," Evan said, "and major in natural history at the College of the Redwoods."

"You can *have* Ferndale," said the president. "In

55

return for a favor. Do you remember an evening — two weeks ago, by your time — when your father finished work on Substance 1000?"

"Yes."

The president, the doctor, and General Rodriguez glanced at each other. Fallon beckoned for a chair, sat down near Evan, and peered at him, his black crystal orbs gleaming. "Just what do you remember about it, my boy?"

"Not a thing. It was just some of Dad's scientific gobbledygook."

"No, no," Dr. Corday corrected sharply. "You only think you've forgotten. Actually, the brain never forgets anything it has recorded, whether we understand it or not. Under proper stimulus, we can pull out of a person's memory anything he ever knew."

"So what you're getting at," Evan said, "is that you want the formula for Substance 1000."

"So that the aged can be young again!" Fallon cried. "Yes, that's it! Will you help? Will you make us young again?"

Evan could feel his heart racing; he saw the surgeon glance at the meters and knew he had picked up on his state of mind.

"Let me point something out to you," he said to the leader. "I've got problems, too. I'm seventeen years old, and I just fell off my planet. But that doesn't matter. I could use a little help myself. All you want is my help in creating a race of super-drones. They walk like people, they talk like people, but they're zombies."

"But, my boy!" said Charlie Fallon, in anguish, his eyes clicking around at the others. "We'd be

young again! Corday estimates my E-Double-A-T —
Estimated Age After Treatment, that is — at forty-
three. I'm actually a hundred and seventy-six."

"Can I ask you something?" Evan said. "When
will you be ready to quit? What's the point of living
forever?"

Fallon shushed a protest from Dr. Corday, and
said:

"We're tiring you, Evan. Now, Jansen, I want him
to have everything he wants, in reason. And nurse,
see to it that you don't blind him — ha-ha! I understand you're his favorite."

Eliza looked down, flustered. "Who told you that,
sir?"

"There are no secrets from Lake House," said the
leader. He sounded jolly, but Evan had the clear
impression that he was issuing a warning. "Would
you like to assist Doctor Corday when he makes the
adjustment to my orbs?" he asked.

"Of course, sir," Eliza said, faintly.

"Then you'll be notified when the work is to be
done."

11

*I*t was the longest and most harrowing day of Eliza's life. She had to work almost two shifts, and did not leave until midnight, when Evan was asleep. She got Jansen's locum to issue her a sandwich to take home, as there were no stores open and she was out of food. She caught a late train and it clanked and bored along underground like an iron mole, carrying her to her station. A lecherous-looking old man leered at her until she laid her stunner in her lap.

Hurrying down the dreary street, she stopped to fill her collapsible water bucket at the community tap. She was worried about Attila, alone for so long. But maybe he had caught a rat or two. Wearily climbing the stairs to her floor, sickened by the reek of stale food and rodents, she thought of how it would have impressed Evan. Could he ever adjust to such a squalid world? How awful to come from a dream of meadows, redwoods, and rivers to what must seem a nightmare of madmen running a hospital! Sighing, she hung her light-cube from a nail beside her door while she groped for her keys. She found one and tried to insert it — but there was no lock. All there was, she saw, was a metal plate covering the seven keyholes. She was locked out! But why? There were no problems with the landlord.

Vexed, she knocked on the door.

"Who is it?" a voice said.

"Eliza Gamble."

The door opened. She saw the small eyes, cold as a ferret's, evil as the rat-infested garbage pit down the block, of General Rodriguez. He held a weapon, but his mouth eased into a grin as he snapped on a light.

"Come in, Eliza. Expecting you, dear."

She saw with anger that the flat had been ransacked. Drawers had been rifled, a chair overturned. "What have you been doing?" she wailed.

"Sorry, Gamble. Rules, rules, rules. Also we decided you needed protection. Hence the new lock. Here's the magnetic key."

Eliza saw somthing that made her whimper. On the bare flooring by the sofa lay the cat, Attila — his head burst open like a melon, his blood and brains on the planking.

"Pity," sighed Rodriguez. "Move him out into the hall, will you? I loathe cats, and when he rubbed against my leg I overreacted."

Eliza stared at him blankly, then used the sandwich wrapper to carry the cat into the hall. She came back and stood waiting, her head down.

"Sit down, Gamble. I know you've had quite a

day, but I need some reassurance about your personal beliefs."

"My *beliefs?* My mind was *sieved* before I was ever accepted at Clark Memorial."

Rodriguez smirked. "Gently, Eliza. Tell me, what do you do with your spare time?"

"Study Seniors nursing." She knew he was way ahead of her, that there was no use holding back. "— And a couple of years ago I started building a miniature of Evan Clark's home."

"Saw it in the closet, love. Very clever work. How did you happen to select it, instead of, say, Charlie Fallon's home?"

"We studied the Clarks in American history. And ever since I was a little girl, I was mystified about where Evan could have vanished to. I had a burning ambition to solve the mystery. I started with the basics of his life. Then I wrote a thesis on Evan's last day. I got a prize for it."

"So that you have a certain special feeling for the young man?"

"Yes. I'm interested in so many of the things that he was. I've practically memorized his diary — his school days, picnics on the Centerville Beach — everything he thought important enough to write down."

Rodriguez was doing a sort of cat's cradle with his bony fingers. He looked queer and ugly, with his long iron gray hair and cheeks with pockets like thumbholes in dough. "Do you know why Charlie wears receptor orbs?" he asked.

"Of course. A mad underground boy threw acid in his face at the opening of a new Puncture Pavilion for Rejuvenal treatment."

"And how do you feel about acts like that?"

Eliza stamped her foot. "This is quite uncalled for! The mere fact that I work at Clark Memorial tells everything about my attitudes. But you're taking the tack that I have some prejudice against the superannuated!"

Rodriguez beamed. "That's the spirit! All I wanted to hear. Because there may be some awkwardness with your young hero."

"Why?"

"We aren't sure he's anxious to cooperate with us."

"He's only been awake a few days. He's still got both feet in his old world. The reanimation should have covered weeks and weeks. Give him time."

"We don't have time. Another thing to consider, Gamble, is that your first allegiance is to President Fallon, not to Evan Clark."

"Politically, not professionally. During working hours, my allegiance is to my patient."

"Fine, fine. As long as some schoolgirl crush doesn't becloud your vision."

"It won't," Eliza said crisply. "My genes, instincts, and credo are a matter of record."

General Rodriguez nodded. "Then we're of one mind. Sorry about the cat, dear."

Eliza wrapped the dead cat in a sheet of paper. She sniffled. "Poor baby!" she said. He had been so lovely. His collar was stained with blood. As she removed it, she remembered that one of the silver studs was a tiny transceiver. Did it still work?

Halfway to the refuse station, under a lofty palm,

she took the collar from the bag and whispered, "Captain!"

"I heard it all, Eliza. I'm sorry about Attila. I'll bring you another cat tomorrow night."

"Should you? They may be watching me now." She wondered why she felt a need to warn him, as though he had something to hide. Yet she had the strong impression that he was on one side of a river, Fallon and his people on the other.

"It's all right. I'll bring it to the hospital tomorrow night," Tuggey's voice said. "I'll be there early. Another rat scare — frightened Jansen out of her wits. . . ."

Eliza went on to the garbage pit in the wide alley down the block. She shot a few menacing red-eyed rats with her laser pistol, and laid the cat's body in the trash. Maybe two weeks hence a scow from the spaceport, where garbage was laserized into fuels and building blocks, would come by to pick up the reeking mass. Or two months. . . .

nother Eliza came and went with brisk efficiency the next morning. She was a little freer with the information today, perhaps because of some high-level decision. She told Evan, as she dusted his pyramid of gold bricks, how fortunate he was to be so wealthy at seventeen.

"You bet, and I'm already putting my wealth to good use," Evan agreed. Standing near the windows, he was using two gold bars as dumbbells as he exercised his shoulder muscles. Then he lay on his back with his arms outstretched and thudded the weights together above his head.

Later, while the nurse made his bed, he stood looking down on the rooftop patterns of the buildings near the hospital. On many of them were tiny gardens. People strolled among the plants.

"Are you Duodecima?" he asked, without turning.

"Yes. Means 'twelfth,' you know."

"Why don't I call you E-12, then?"

"If you wish."

"What kind of buildings are those down there?"

"Residential complexes for Seniors. Most of the tenants held important jobs or performed some kind of special service."

"Like military?"

E-12 plumped his pillows. "No, no. Invented television games, for instance."

Evan turned. "Important service? You're kidding!"

"Not at all. Boredom is the most serious social problem of all; we had a patient here last month who'd invented a television game called *Down You Go*. He got fantastic royalties out of it! But he, well, he's gone on now."

"Died of boredom, maybe?" Evan suggested.

The nurse peeked at the window in the door, and apparently decided to answer, in a whisper. "There's a baffling epidemic called Logardo's syndrome. Just going like wildfire! The Committee of Thirteen is working on it." She suddenly sounded like a medical student. "It's characterized by anomie, distractibility, hypomotility, affective lethargy, or lack of psychomotor function —"

"In short," said Evan, "terminal boredom." And he gazed down on the intricate warrens of buildings that gave off, like dust from a beaten rug, the atmosphere of ennui.

"So," he mused, "Doctor Clark's Golden Medical Discovery can keep you alive, but not make you like it."

The nurse tilted her head as she studied him. "I don't always understand you, Evan...."

He shrugged, took up a stance like a bowler, and slid one of his golden ingots toward the wall at the end of the room. It glided over the carpet, coming to rest just short of the golden pyramid. "Bingo," he said.

At sixteen hundred the door opened and Eliza Tertia hurried in with an enormous cat in her arms. It was gray, with tiger stripes, and black lines running back from the corners of its amber eyes. Evan saw the tips of tearing fangs beneath its upper lip. But despite its look of ferocity, he could hear the low rumble of a purr.

"Tertia!" exclaimed E-12. "What *is* that?"

Evan sat up.

"Captain Tuggey gave him to me," Eliza said smugly. "Isn't he wonderful? He's over the hill for commercial ratting, he said, but he'll certainly raise heck with the rodents around Harley Mansions."

The other nurse stroked the cat, shrugged, and said, "Ta-ta, Tertia. All yours." She departed.

Despite her pleasure in the cat, Evan noticed that Eliza looked wan as she sat by him and got to her bookwork. He took the cat onto his lap and examined it.

"Kaffir, isn't he? But about twice normal size. Must weigh nine kilograms!"

She explained about Captain Tuggey, about his armies of pest exterminators and his cats, while Evan checked the cat like a veterinarian. He knew he was being given another glimpse into the world of 2164 — a world without pesticides, and rich in pests.

"I wouldn't be surprised if this Kaffir cat had bobcat blood," he said. "Wouldn't think they'd cross, but maybe Tuggey's found a way, if he's such a dynamite breeder. What's this guy doing here? Rats in Clark's memorial?"

"Captain Tuggey thinks they're coming in by a utility duct. He's inspecting them tonight. Let me hold the cat now, while you lie back for the meter checks."

Evan watched her. "Eliza," he said, "you look terrible."

"Changing to a new shift is a little hard. But I'm as healthy as a horse."

"Even horses get sick." He studied her in profile. She not only looked pallid, but worried. A sudden emotion drove into him like a rusty nail, painful and breathtaking. He knew what was wrong with her.

"How much sleep did you get?" he asked.

"Well, I didn't leave here till quite late," she said.

"And then what did you do?"

"Why, I went home." Eliza's gray eyes widened, and she pointed at the meters. "Evan, do you feel all right? Your signs are just ridiculous! Pulse rate up, blood pressure elevated —"

"What's his name?" Evan asked. He knew he was being irrational, that it was probably just another aspect of reanimation. But he was positive there was a boy in her life; or, worse, a man.

"Captain Tuggey's? Bill, I think. Why?"

"Is he your man-friend? That's how come the gift of a cat?"

Eliza laughed in embarrassment. "Oh," she said. "I see what you're getting at. No, we nurses don't date."

66

"Why not?" He took the cat and carried it down the room, stroking it.

"Well, because we're a little bit like that cat, we Elizas. We're clones, bred for a special purpose, which is nursing. A nurse with her mind on romance is not going to have her mind on work. We go back to a famous nurse named Eliza Smith. She was totally devoted to her calling, never married, had no friends except those in the profession. We are cells of her cells, carbon copies of her genes."

"You mean you've never had a boyfriend?" He gazed across the darkening dome and saw the amber haze thickening. It reminded him of nitric acid fumes steaming in a chemist's retort.

"No. No boyfriend, Evan."

"And therefore, if I understand you, I'm just a case, too."

She looked at the door, then whispered in anxiety, "A very *special* case! I don't quite understand my feelings myself. But I studied you in school. I did a paper on you. Actually it's one reason I was picked for your case, because I was interested in you even before you'd been found. Um, professionally interested, you see."

"You mean that while I was lying there like a frozen fish stick, people were doing papers on me?"

"At least I was."

"Then when I get out of here," Evan said soberly, "why can't we date? Is there any law against it? If there is, let's break it."

Eliza sighed. "This is a very unprofessional conversation we're having," she said. "I can't really say, and please don't insist on an answer, because a no would be bad for you, and a yes might be bad for me — Jansen, you know."

A bell rang. A voice rasped:

"Nurse Eliza Tertia, pick up your patient's tray."

13

*E*liza had just disposed of Evan's tray — he had eaten much better than usual — when a hall speaker rattled.

"Nurse Eliza Tertia to office."

Now, Eliza supposed, the Dragon will have some bitter comment to make about her conversation with Evan. For no doubt Jansen had been listening avidly. If only this were a world like Evan's! What would they do on a "date" in Ferndale? Her studies had supplied a little of this information, yet there were many blanks.

She was still daydreaming about it as she entered Colonel Jansen's office. With the Dragon was an ancient female Guppy, a lumpy old woman in a bright floral print dress cut like a tent, who had a jaw like a bulldog's. The old woman rose from a chair when she saw Eliza enter. She wore a purple wig and had plastered on enough powder base to cover her Guppy effect.

"This is Sherrill Leffler," Jansen said. "Nurse Eliza Tertia will take you to Evan, Mrs. Leffler."

"Oh, fantastic! Oh, I can't believe this!" said the old woman.

"I don't understand — a visitor?" said Eliza.

"I was his girlfriend!" the old thing said archly. "I'm mentioned in the biographies of the family. Take me to Evan, nurse. Right now!"

She seized Eliza's hand and began hauling her into the corridor. But Eliza hung back, gazing at Jansen with pained entreaty.

"Is it wise, Colonel?" she beseeched.

Jansen's face clouded slightly, and she murmured, "The order comes from the top."

"Which way? Which way?" Mrs. Leffler was bleating.

Eliza led off, slightly nauseated. "Charlie came to our flat himself!" the old woman said. "With his palace guards and General Rodriguez and everything. He said Evan's needing support. And that he's not very cooperative. Is that true? Is he balking?"

"About what?"

"Substance 1000, of course. Where's your brain? It's all anybody talks about anymore, isn't it? Young again? *And the answer is right there in his head!* Charlie said the Committee and Doctor Corday will probably have it ready in no time, and we'll turn back the clock!"

"You're too young to fret about old age," Eliza said lightly. "Here we are. I'd better prepare —"

But Mrs. Leffler gave the door guard on his pulpit a peremptory wave and banged through the door.

Eliza followed. Evan was lying on the bed, hands behind his head, but he sat up, frowning as the woman approached.

"Evan!" she shrieked. "Don't you remember me? I'm Sherrill Leffler — Sherrill Dobson, that was! I was a cheerleader — and you — Oh, look at you! You haven't changed at all, Moose! You're beautiful."

Eliza watched Evan rise slowly to his feet; in his face numbness and politeness struggled with horror. He tried to turn away as the old woman planted a big kiss on his mouth. She stood back triumphantly and beamed at him.

"Aren't you the one! The most famous person in the world!"

Evan slipped her grasp and went to stand near the window. The city was dark, lights puncturing the blackness below.

"I'm a freak, Sherrill," he said. "Hawkins did me in. Froze me like a Popsicle."

"But if he hadn't, you'd be — you'd be — like Rusty and me." Suddenly the old woman was weeping.

"Hey, don't," Evan pleaded. "Look, you want a couple of gold bars?"

Sobbing, she shook her head. Wiped her nose. "No, we've got plenty of money — the Seniors Sufficiency Law, you know. Plenty of everything but youth. And you'll help us, won't you, Moose? Make us young again?"

Eliza looked away as Evan glanced at her in desperation. "Sure," he said.

"Charlie Fallon says you can, if you want to."

"I don't know whether I can or not, Sherrill."

Evan shrugged. "He's banking on my remembering a lot of stuff I didn't even understand."

The old woman placed her hand atop her purple wig. "But it's all right up there — in your brain! And they're going to search it. . . ."

Eliza shivered, and again saw Evan glance at her. "Sounds like fun," he said.

"Mrs. Leffler, please return to the office," the loudspeaker squawked. "Mrs. Leffler to the office."

Eliza led the sobbing old woman away. "You don't know —" Mrs. Leffler choked, "what it's like — to see a boy who loved you — see yourself in his face —"

Eliza could imagine, and she thought it monstrous that it should have been permitted to happen. As far as she could see, Charlie was doing everything he could to turn Evan against the Guppies.

She hurried back to Evan's room, worried over the effect the meeting might have had on him. She was surprised to find him building a small house with gold bricks, as a child might construct one of blocks. He seemed unaware of her for a time, and she grew worried about shock.

"Evan?" she said, standing over him.

He stood up, and sighed deeply. "What a shocker!" he muttered. "She was the cutest girl in school — And now — I suppose she's had kids, lived a full life, been married a hundred eighty years — "

Eliza anxiously trailed him around the room as he moved from gold pile to window to bedside table to bed. She was still watching for signs of shock — pallor, a drop in blood pressure.

"Lie down," she said. "I'd like to check something."

He stretched out, pulled the cat to his side, and scratched it behind the ears. He heard the nurse gasp. Then she giggled.

"Oh — I was getting the cat's respiration and heartbeat! Let me have him a minute —"

While she made her notes, he muttered. She paid more attention to what he said than to what she was writing.

". . . That's the point, isn't it, Eliza?" he said, sounding puzzled. "She's done everything we're supposed to do. What's left? Why is she worrying about the next two hundred years?"

Eliza gave the huge cat back to him. Evan's respiration was still too fast, his pulse bounding. "Are they all like that?" Evan asked her. " 'Tired of living, and scared of dying,' as the old song says?"

Eliza tapped her lips. "Let's talk about something else. Your owl — remember it?"

"How did you know about it?"

"In the biographies. Your father let it go free."

"And I imagine it found a mate, and raised a couple of clutches a year. Then a hawk or fox or something got it. But what if my old man had put it on Rejuvenal? It might have lived fifty years, lost all its feathers and claws. . . . It's not natural. I did a report on a book by a gerontologist last year — a hundred and eighty-one years ago, that is. And he said, 'The goal of medicine is not to prolong life. It's to improve the quality of life.' Are these old people enjoying life?"

"I don't know, Evan," Eliza murmured.

Evan sat on the edge of the bed. "I'd better get my act together, Eliza," he sighed.

"Your act?"

"What I'm going to do. I may refuse to help. I probably will refuse. Things are bad enough already."

His jaw was set. She got an inkling of why they called him Moose. She cut in hastily, "Well, I don't think any big decisions have to be made just —"

The door opened. Eliza watched Jansen glide in, deadpan, followed by Dr. Corday. The doctor's face revealed no emotion or any particular interest. As usual he was dressed in pale blue, the color of an iceberg, and his green eyes had the deadness of glass. He carried a medical probe in one gloved hand, and for some reason it shocked Eliza, who had heard whispered stories about his experiments on cats and convicts.

Jansen moved a chair to the bedside, and Corday sat down and gave Evan a remote smile. "Well, young Clark, I thought we'd have a chat this evening."

Evan looked at the probe and frowned. Jansen turned to Eliza. "Go keep an eye on that Tuggey man. He has a gold pass, but he doesn't own the place, as he sometimes seems to think."

14

*E*liza went directly to the nurses' lounge and poured herself a cup of tea. She did not know where Tuggey was, but the easiest way to find out was to scan the monitors in the briefing room next door. So she went in and glanced at the almost identical pictures in the wall. The full length of the corridors could be viewed here. A nurse was walking down a hall; the guard before Evan's room was doing a puzzle, apparently; she saw a male aide pushing a cart of laundry. Suddenly she choked on her tea and stared.

Tuggey in Zone Blue! Apparently — oh, good Lord! — coming out of the elevator to the Committee chambers!

She stepped to the wall and her finger stabbed at a button in the center of a red circle: the general alarm. But she held back. It would bring guards, get

Captain Tuggey in serious trouble. She would talk to him herself. That madman!

She set her tea on a desk and angrily hurried down the hall. . . .

The king of the ratters was placing his cat in its cage when she arrived. "Captain Tuggey!" she whispered furiously.

He looked at her, seeming dazed. His face was waxen. "What's up?"

"I saw you on the monitor!" Eliza hissed.

He gazed numbly at her, then took something from his pocket. It appeared to be a coin. "Do you know what this is?" he asked.

She took it and saw that it was a cameo of the face of Walter Stevens Clark — that it would fit into the intaglio of the elevator button beside the door.

She handed it back. "Get rid of it! Listen to me, Captain —"

But he had placed it against the wall, and the car doors parted and revealed a small car, uncarpeted and sterile-looking. He motioned her inside, but she shook her head. Suddenly, as quick as one of his cats, he placed one hand over her mouth, the other behind her head, thumb and forefinger finding painful nerves, and in a second he had dragged her into the car.

The door closed. She struggled. "I'm sorry!" he said. "I want you to see this. It will help you to decide what to do about Evan. It's your responsibility as his nurse."

His hand dropped away. The car was rising slowly. Too astonished, too shocked to speak, the nurse stared at him.

76

"I don't believe this!" she gasped, as the car halted. "This is absolutely the most —"

The gray doors parted on a small gray vestibule. He gestured. "More! We'll be back in two minutes."

He stepped out, but she stubbornly remained in the car. As she watched, he used the coin again to open a door. Through it, she saw a laboratory — computers, glass vessels, pumps, and tubes — and beyond a half-height partition, what looked like a richly furnished boardroom. On the paneled walls were pictures of Dr. Clark, Charlie Fallon, Evan, and a few noted Seniors. But the partition hid the Committee table.

Eliza shuddered. She did not at once realize why she was going so queasy. Something about the look of the lab . . . It was a familiar setup. She had it! In medical school she had seen similar arrangements. And in that case the large glass vessels must be filled with blood. An advanced heart-and-lung setup . . .

". . . Yes, it's blood," the ratter said. "Come and meet the Committee. . . ."

She let him draw her through the laboratory, past the whirring, muttering computers. A glance at the network of glass tubing, of pumps, tiny turbines, and a domed glass fountain pumping dark liters of blood. The ratter held her arm, steadying her as they went around the partition. Eliza went cold and dizzy, as if she were falling down an elevator shaft.

At the far end of the boardroom, taking up half the total floor space, was a horseshoe-shaped table. In the middle of the open space, facing the table, was a desk. Thirteen chairs were arranged about the horseshoe. A single chair was placed before the desk.

The Committee of Thirteen appeared to be in session, but the members' eyes were closed. There were four women and nine men. Eliza uttered a moan, and instantly all the eyes flew open and stared at her. Then a babble of voices broke out, each coming from a small speaker beside a Committee member — toneless, inflectionless computer voices. Brainwave-actuated artificial voices, counterfeits of human voices, with male and female tones.

"Help us. Help us. Have you come to turn us off? Oh, please. God will bless you."

Eliza leaned against the captain, his arm about her to keep her from collapsing on the floor. But she could not obliterate from her mind what she had seen:

Thirteen heads mounted in black bases on the walnut half-ring, like marble heads atop Greek columns. Tubes of blood and serum, a spaghettilike network tangled beneath the table and passing through the partition to the life-support machines. The heads were shaven, even the women's, but the men's cheeks wore stubbly beards, many of them gray. One head was black. The sounds came from speakers actuated by their brain waves.

"Turn us off. You cannot leave us. Have you come to save us? If you do not kill us, we will report that you have been here. We are their prisoners but now you are ours."

Eliza looked at them, her vision blurring. The faces were pallid. The eyes stared in anguish, like those of martyrs.

"Doctor Giddings — is that you, sir?" Captain Tuggey asked. "I've seen your picture."

"Of course it's me."

"Yes it's him."

"Don't you know me?"

"I'm Doctor Opal Snyder. Break the machines."

"I'm McCawley — please — in the name of God —"

"One at a time, please," Tuggey said, and drew a deep breath. "I'll help you, if you help us. Tell us what happened. Doctor Giddings, please answer."

The central head, showing the gaunt anguish of a medieval Christ, spoke with its metal larynx.

"We were too important to risk being lost to accidents or illness. Corday persuaded Fallon to decapitate us. Heads don't get sick or have mishaps."

"What do you do here?"

"We work on Substance 1000. Voice-operated computers. Not making much progress. But Corday promised us death soon. Is it true that they've found Evan Clark?"

Eliza leaned against the partition, cold and weak. Only a monster like Corday would think of it. Only a lunatic would do it. Another voice — coming from the speaker beside the black head she recognized as that of Dr. McCawley, a neurosurgeon — spoke to them.

"They promised to return our bodies. But we've computerized the possibility. It can't be done. Free us, oh God, free us."

Tuggey slumped into the chair at the desk and regarded the heads. "I'll help. But I've got to free Evan Clark first. You wouldn't want him to join you, would you?"

"If it will free us," said McCawley's voice. "Anything. Any price."

Dr. Giddings' voice came again. "I have two hundred thousand new Clarks hidden in my old office. I'll tell you where if you will disconnect us."

"But if we do that, they'll immediately suspect me, and then I can't help Evan."

"You can't help Evan anyway. Help us."

"We can get him out of here," Tuggey said.

A woman's voice clattered out, so rapidly the words were almost incomprehensible: "It can look like an accident — a rat gnawing through a main tube — immediate coagulation of our blood. Corday said there's been rats."

"All right!" Tuggey agreed. "But not until tomorrow night."

The black head retorted: "No. Tonight. Or I'll report you."

"That won't help you, Doctor," the ratter said calmly. A babble of voices. "Filings in a turbine bearing!" "Oil leak!" "Electrical malfunction!"

"The rat idea is best. I'll bring one tomorrow night, and leave it here after I cut the tube with rats' teeth. But if you expose me, then I can't help you. We're checkmated."

"How do we know you'll come back?" Dr. Giddings' voice asked.

Tuggey stood up, smiling. "Because you have me in your power. If I don't come back, you'll expose me and they'll arrest me. But then you'll have to go on suffering forever. So we've got to help each other. I've got to destroy you to protect myself. Do you want to decide now? We've got to leave. *Aye*, you cooperate with me. *Nay*, you call a guard. Vote."

"Aye!" "Aye!" "Aye!" the speakers squawked. There was not a single nay — fortunate, thought Eliza, since one head could summon the guards!

"I promise to return tomorrow night," the ratter said, and then, with morbid humor: "After all, doctors — extermination is my business!"

There was a strange medley of sounds, like chickens cackling, which Eliza supposed was electronic laughter; and she saw several of the heads smile.

They hurried from the chamber of horrors.

15

They were paging Eliza when she emerged from the elevator in tears. "Awful! Awful!" she moaned.

"Eliza Tertia to patient's room," a speaker rasped.

She leaned against the wall, white-faced, sniffling and dabbing at her eyes. "I can't go like this! They'd know in a minute."

"Breathe deeply. Just be quiet and do what they tell you. They won't notice anything, because they're all wrapped up in Evan."

She started taking deep breaths. "Cosmas help me! I'll try."

"I'll meet you tomorrow night, as near twenty-two hundred as possible. Be in his room, alone, getting him ready for the night."

"How can I promise anything, Captain? It's up to Jansen where I'll be."

"I'll handle Jansen. Go back to Evan now, and keep breathing deeply."

He picked up his carrying cage and walked away. Still wobbly, Eliza ventured into the main corridor and started slowly for Evan's room, dabbing at her eyes. She would never forget the grisly sight. . . . "Steady, nurse!" she said to herself. By the time she reached the guard's pulpit beside Evan's door, she was giddy from hyperventilation. Her head swam. She looked blankly at the door guard, who said:

"They've been calling you, nurse."

"Yes, I heard them." She went into the room. Dr. Corday, slim, elegant, and surly, was standing by Evan's bed. Since Jansen was not there, Eliza presumed she must have paged her from the office.

"Where were you?" Corday asked impatiently.

When Eliza hesitated, he said angrily, "Never mind! Stylus and block. Hurry up." He waited while she got the writing materials. "Tests for tomorrow morning," he dictated. "Deep-scan in the fissure of Sylvius. Full hematocrit. CDR and iodalite probes. Results to be on my desk by noon."

He walked out.

Evan lay with his arms crossed under his head, his eyes smoky with anger. "One way or another," he said levelly, "I'm walking out of here tomorrow, Eliza."

"Nonsense, Evan. You have the best medical help in the world. Soon it will all be over and you can leave."

She flipped to a blank sheet and wrote two words in a shaky scrawl. She moved to adjust his pillow, and, as she did so, laid the page beside him. Evan looked at it. Eliza knew Corday was probably watching and listening on the guard's monitor.

". . . Fantastic administrator and the best brain man in the world," Eliza crooned, as though she were settling one of her old patients. "The nurses all love him, and our old ladies are his slaves!"

"I'm not his slave," Evan growled. He read what she had written: *Tomorrow night.*

"But it's *just* a few simple tests, Evan. Please?"

"Well — they'd better be simple."

"Thank you! And now it's time for you pills, and then a wonderful sleep. . . ."

When she left a few moments later, Dr. Corday was walking away from the guard's pulpit.

16

*E*van got up early and watched a gray dawn wash over the grimy 0-2 dome. The few Guppies down in the street moved slowly, like lizards on a hot day. The impression of a suffocating boredom rose from the streets and buildings like dust. He pictured Sherrill living down there somewhere, playing lawn games and participating in television contests. What a gruesome creature she had become! To see the peppy little cheerleader transformed into a revolting caricature of herself . . . !

E-12 brought his breakfast. "There's some real orange juice today," she said. He sipped suspiciously, then gulped it down, and a few moments later his vision began to blur. For a half hour thereafter, he had no awareness of what went on. When he came to, E-12 said primly:

"Sorry, Evan. We had to do it to insure your co-operation."

He was still groggy. "For the tests? I already said I'd do them, didn't I?"

"Yes, but the prepping — you see, we had to shave your head."

His hand wandered up and found his skull as slick and skinned as an onion. One of these days, Corday! he thought bitterly. One of these days!

The tests were conducted in a small examination room with the blue-and-white decor of a bedroom. They were simple and painless and over in minutes. Corday completed a final eye test and straightened up.

"All right. Back you go. Everything normal." No expression on his face, the skin of which was drawn in thin wrinkles over the jellied flesh and skull like model airplane paper unevenly stretched.

"I've got a question," Evan said.

"Certainly."

"What do the tests show?"

"What I told you — that everything is fine."

"So when can I leave?"

"Five days. A week," said the surgeon. "I'll work out a plan with Charlie."

"If I don't see him again," Evan said, "tell him I said good-bye."

Bleak smile. "Thank you."

Afterward, he regretted having said it. Corday was no idiot. He might computerize the remark and get a printout reporting that Evan was going to escape tonight. . . .

When Eliza came at ten minutes after sixteen

hundred, E-12 said, "The leopard never changes her spots. I'd hoped to get off on time, Tertia."

"Sorry, Duo! But I stopped to catch a butterfly for Evan. He had a marvelous collection, you know."

"No, I didn't. How fascinating."

As the other nurse left, Eliza took a notebook from her purse and opened it carefully. A large brownish butterfly had been pressed between two pages. She saw the guard peering in.

"What variety is it?" she asked.

He noticed that her fingers were trembling. He glanced into her eyes, then studied the butterfly. "Viceroy. Nice one."

"I found it in some weeds near my place. Look at the antennae. . . ."

When he peered more closely, she slipped the butterfly down the page, and he saw that the brown-and-white wings had concealed some hairlike writing. *Trust the one who comes.*

He sank back, stunned. Was he really getting out? The risks seemed fantastic. He realized then that he must be in great danger, or she'd never let him attempt to escape.

"Very nice," he said.

At seventeen-thirty she brought his dinner. He had been exercising, and was sweating, but feeling stronger. Every day since the frost melted he had felt life rising through him like sap. Now, invigorated by the exercise, he wanted to run through the woods and yell. Chop wood and climb a tree.

Nineteen hundred.

Eliza scribbled in a notebook, studied his charts. Corday popped in.

"Weigh the patient," he said.

Eliza ran a green laser beam over him and looked at a dial on the instrument.

"Eighty-four-point-zero-nine kilos," she reported.

"You will not work tomorrow, Gamble," Corday said.

Eliza's fists clenched. "But I'm not taking days off during Evan's re-an. Colonel Jansen —"

"I want you to spend the day relaxing. On the following day you'll assist me on the adjustment of Charlie's receptor orbs."

"Oh. Thank you, Doctor. I wonder — could you help me get a pass to visit the Clark Museum in Ferndale tomorrow, then? I could take an official slider up —"

"Negative on that, Gamble."

Eliza looked down.

"Here's something that might amuse you," Corday said to Evan, with an aloof smile. He handed him a metal ball about the size of a baseball. "See how fast you can take that apart and put it together. Time him, Gamble."

He departed.

Evan sat cross-legged on the bed with the gleaming sphere, which was light in weight and almost free of scratches. Now, what? He made out nearly imperceptible scorings, and recalled similar puzzles. After a few moments he was able to slide a keylike piece from the sphere, then another and another: intricate bars, slots, and angles.

At last it lay before him, more than a dozen complex parts. "Time!"

"Six minutes twenty-two seconds."

But reassembling the ball was much harder. He began to believe the infuriating parts had the capability of changing shape; then quite suddenly they began to go together. "Twenty-eight minutes thirteen seconds!" Eliza said.

"You try," Evan said. He saw the craggy-faced guard glance in curiously.

Eliza's fingers were quick and clever. She dismantled the ball in four minutes and a few seconds, reassembled it in less than ten. She showed him some key moves and he improved his performance.

After a few more tries he was able to break it down in less than a minute and reassemble it in a minute and a half.

"It certainly makes the time pass, doesn't it?" Eliza said, breathlessly; and Evan saw that it was almost twenty-two hundred! "I wonder how fast the guard can do it?" the nurse said.

"Try him," suggested Evan.

"I will. But now you should rest; then I'll tuck you in for the night. Lie back. Think good thoughts. Here, I'll dim the light. . . ."

She turned off all the lights except a lamp in a far corner. His bed was in shadow. Eliza went out. Through the window he could see her dark hair as she talked to the guard. She came back for a stopwatch. "He's going to try to beat you," she said, and giggled. But her eyes were frightened.

The door closed softly.

Evan lay propped on the bed. Dimly he could see his vital-signs meters. His pulse rate was nearly ninety.

Trust the one who comes. . . .

From where? Through the door? From the closet?

He heard a sharp tap on his window, and twisted around to stare. Something was hanging there in the darkness — a black bundle. Then he saw that it was the upper portion of a man's body, waist to head, and that he was clad entirely in black, and was masked.

17

The guard jockeyed the last slug into the puzzle and said, "Time, nurse!"

Eliza giggled. "Twenty-eight minutes. Oh, Brumitt!"

The guard groaned. "Cripes! Well, I had to go and leave high school when I was only sixty-four." He was a hulking man of well over a hundred, with a black wig like artificial turf, and heavy brows locking above his nose.

Eliza saw a man coming from a spur of hall toward them, a familiar, burly figure moving slowly and carrying a cage and a sack. "Try it again?" she asked the guard.

"No. I get my break pretty soon. Look who's here!" he said as the ratter dropped the sack near the pulpit. "How's the ratting tonight, Captain?"

"Caught two red zingers up in Valhalla. What you got there?" Tuggey was breathing hard.

"Puzzle. Take it apart, put it together. Try it. Nothing to it." Brumitt winked at Eliza.

But just then a speaker grated. "Captain Tuggey to the briefing station."

"Strange," said Tuggey. "That's Jansen. Just left her. By the way, here's a worming pill for the cat I gave you."

He gave her a tiny envelope. On it she saw the words: *Place under cat's tongue. Stat.* She blinked. *Stat* was prescription talk for *at once.* So the pill was for her.

As she entered Evan's room, she placed the tiny lozenge under her tongue. She was shocked to see that Evan had indeed vanished! She closed her eyes, trying not to break down, then tore the envelope to bits and flushed them down the toilet. Already she felt the drug in her bloodstream; her ears rang and the room went out of focus.

. . . In the hall the guard heard her exclaim: "Evan?" And a moment later: "Evan! Are you in the bathroom?"

And then she screamed.

Eliza lay on the bed. Five other persons moved about the room. Eliza had fainted, and Brumitt had stretched her out on the bed and called Jansen, who had summoned Dr. Corday. Corday and Jansen were observing her vital signs.

"Long time coming around," murmured Corday.

Head Nurse Colonel Jansen, thin as an eel, her icy features flushed for once, stood glaring down at Eliza. "She's faking it! I've known patients who could consciously slow their pulses and lower their blood pressure."

"Not for this length of time. Gamble?"

Eliza's eyelids fluttered. The guard, sitting deject-edly on a chair, said, "She probably don't know any more than I do. She was with me when it happened." He repeated, at Corday's command, what he had already told them of the disappearance.

General Rodriguez, sniffing about the room, sud-denly seized the canvas sack at Captain Tuggey's feet and emptied its contents on the floor. It con-tained two dead rats, the remnants of a sandwich, a light-cube, and a pair of gloves.

"Eliza Tertia!" Jansen shook the nurse angrily. The dark head flopped on the pillow.

"Let it go," said Corday. "Why don't you call in again for a report, Rodriguez?" he said.

The security boss punched some buttons on a hand console and a picture formed on a wall screen. It was of a large office with desks, monitors, and some computers, Rodriguez punched another button and the camera zoomed into a lean, uniformed man at a central computer console.

"Any news?" Rodriguez said.

"There was very light traffic at all air locks. Gar-bage sliders passed through Ecluse Barbara and Ecluse Karen in that time interval. We've asked for the P.I.N.s of the men who were driving the garbage sliders, but you know how much cooperation we get at the scow port."

A chime resounded and the picture tore and was immediately replaced with a new one — the big, sleep-rumpled visage of President Fallon, a couple of men whispering excitedly behind him. One hand touched his left receptor orb, and his face showed anguish.

"Yes, Rodriguez," he said. "I was asleep. Maybe you'd better give it to me again."

"Evan was kidnapped between twenty-two hundred and twenty-two thirty," Rodriguez reported. "They cut through the window with a laser. But the circular outtake was in the room. Evan must have been lowered somehow."

"Fifty-four floors?" asked Fallon.

"It's possible."

"Then how did they get in? Wasn't the guard on duty?"

"Absolutely. They came down on a line from Valhalla, apparently."

"Was any nonstaff person up there?"

Rodriguez beckoned Tuggey, who came over promptly.

"I was, Mr. President. I'm Tuggey, the exterminator. . . ."

"Exterminator! What a hell of a time to use that word!" groaned Fallon. "They'll kill Evan! Ad Astra! What were you doing up there?"

"Trapping rats. Head Nurse Jansen called my office today. I was in the presence of Colonel Jansen herself. She saw me catch two rats in the dining room."

Fallon rubbed his face with both hands, and let them drop. "Rodriguez," he said, "invoke the Omnibus Seniors Search Warrant we were discussing. Get word out that we'd like to see some volunteer search parties organized among our people. With the warrant, any Senior can go anywhere. Might turn up some Juvie cells if nothing else."

"I'd better get the Seniors Senate to make it sound

constitutional," Rodriguez reflected. "But absolutely, Mr. President."

Fallon took a deep breath. The anvil-chimed visage rose, and his fly-eyes gazed at the group in the hospital room.

"All kneel."

Surprised, they looked at each other, then knelt on the floor.

"At times like this," intoned the leader, "the strongest of us are in the hands of our computers and our security police. Whisper the smallest clue to your computer; trust Central Security, take them into your very hearts, even if it involves betraying a loved one. Rise, please."

Fallon winced as he finished, and touched his faulty receptor orb. Corday spoke urgently.

"Charlie, the work on your orbs just won't wait! The nerve may be deteriorating. I'm going to do the work tomorrow."

"All right, my boy. And bring Nurse Gamble along to assist you. I'd like to ask her some questions."

The vision faded, theatrically; the screen went black.

"Eliza is conscious now," Dr. Corday said. "What happened, Gamble?"

Eliza had been helped to sit on the edge of the bed. Her face in her hands, she rocked back and forth. "Evan was almost asleep when I left the room. When I came back, he was gone. They say I fainted. I don't recall that. I only remember seeing his empty bed. The sight of it —"

Jansen thrust her face into Eliza's. "You're lying, you little snit!"

Corday said, "Oh, now, Jansen. It was a real faint, no doubt about it. You saw the meters. It won't help to start shouting at each other. Come on — let's all go to work."

Eliza became aware that General Rodriguez was watching her, his sardonic features amused. He smiled, a between-us smile, and it made his narrow fox-face and salt-ball eyes more evil.

He knows, he knows! she thought.

18

*E*van was dropping like a runaway elevator,
supported by a thread so fine he could not
even see it. He giggled with exhilaration,
kicking away from the wall whenever he
approached it too closely, spinning, revolving, swinging out on a graceful arc. Hundreds of feet of empti-
ness below him; but the man in black had said:

"Friends are waiting below. Dangerous, but the
lesser of two evils, I guarantee you. Off you go!"

With a laser torch, he had cut a big circle out of
Evan's window and entered, laying the glass on the
floor, had rigged a hang-bar in place, and motioned
Evan to climb out. Evan had lingered long enough to
ask:

"Will Eliza be all right?"

"Never mind Eliza. Hurry!"

Now the sounds from the alley below were louder,
the air was warmer, and he had the impression a

diving bird must have as it approached the water, that of a solid substance below. Then he became suddenly lighter, and realized he was slowing; presently he was simply hanging in space.

He looked down.

A few yards below, in an alley, a boxy white truck was parked. Two workmen were hurling bags of hospital trash into the back of it. They looked up. One continued to work, but the other came to stand beneath Evan, who was now slowly reeling down like a spider. His feet touched the pavement. He staggered and caught himself.

They looked at each other.

The garbage man was about Evan's age, dark-skinned and stocky, with the features of an American Indian. He wore a dirty jump suit, heavy gloves, and a red helmet.

"Climb in back with the trash," he said quickly. "Pull on the jump suit you'll find and take your place on the step beside my buddy. My name's Indio. His is Corky. No last names. You're Stan."

Evan scrambled in with the trash. He found a dirty jump suit, a black helmet, a pair of gloves, and some heavy boots. There was an ID badge clipped to one pocket. The garbage truck moved away, not on wheels but on what felt like a silent cushion of air. He crawled out to join Corky, a very tall youth with a dirty face and red hair. The truck turned left, swept on, turned right, and lost itself in winding streets. Then it slowed and settled, and Evan heard machinery clanking. Ahead of them he saw a wall of translucent plastic, a sort of curtain hanging down from the dark sky: the wall of the oxygen dome.

A skull-faced Guppy in uniform went to the driver's side and looked Indio over, then came back and inspected Corky and Evan. He motioned them on.

A rush of air, a clank, and they were in a different atmosphere, one that smelled musty. They glided onto an express ramp at one side of a dingy street and moved on at high speed.

The neighborhoods they passed fascinated Evan. Most of the buildings were darkened for the night; beyond a certain point there were no streetlamps. The lights in a few dilapidated flats were yellow, like old-fashioned oil lamps. People were lying on mats on the sidewalks.

"Where are we going?" he asked.

"Municipal scow ports."

"Where are we now?"

"Harley Mansions area, Juvenile residential. Be quiet. Your picture's on your badge, and your name is Stan Tully, if anybody asks."

Evan straightened, peering down the street. "Harley Mansions is where that nurse lives!"

"Quiet," Corky warned.

Evan took in all he could of the zone, a depressing one indeed. Sounds and pictures rushed at him, faster than he could sort them. He saw dismal living quarters through windows — appalling, most of them. People sleeping in alleys and on sidewalks. Once they flashed above a shouting ring of men surrounding two bloodied figures; one had a knife, the other a chunk of concrete. Beyond them a small gang of police were approaching with tubular weapons.

They were out of the city then and in a field where

lines of skeletal towers loomed, each with an upturn dish at the top, a garden of steel daisies.

Later there were dark bogs beside the way, and the gases of rotting vegetables. Hydroponic vegetable gardens?

One hundred eighty years compressed into twenty minutes.

Corky offered his hand. "They said it couldn't be done!"

"Where are we?"

He pointed. Something like a skyrocket was arching into the night; another and another went up, strange and beautiful. "Space scows," he said. "Nuclear garbage for Outer Nowhere, riding out on laser launchers. We'll dump our trash at the treatment station and go on to our quarters."

"What happens next?"

"That gets into strategy. I'm just a combat soldier."

They reached a black wall. A guard in a tower raked the truck with a spotlight. He and Indio talked; the gate slid back and they entered. A sign pointed left: NUCLEAR. Another pointed right: OTHER. They swept right.

"They actually shoot nuclear waste into space?" Evan asked.

"New idea of the president's. He promised to get rid of two hundred years of nuke-waste in four years."

The truck stopped behind a building, and Indio rotated it into place before a conveyor belt and let it settle to earth. Refuse began to discharge automatically onto the conveyor belt and disappear into the building. Bitter fumes hung in the air.

Indio silently led the way down the line of trucks, beating his gloves together. They cut through a truck park toward a group of ramshackle buildings, most of them dark. Indio unlocked a battered shack and they went inside.

19

A big, florid man in stained work clothes was waiting in the dark, sitting upright in a straight-backed chair, when Indio turned on a light. He had slanting eyebrows and a friendly grin.

"Everything copacetic?" he asked.

"Smooth as a baby's back!" Corky replied.

Evan regarded the man wearily as he came toward him with a penlight instrument in his hand. "They call me Buzz, Evan. I'm a physician by training, but a street vendor by presidential decree. I'm out of favor with Charlie Fallon. I'd like to make some tests to see exactly where you are in your recovery. All right?"

Evan nodded. He sat on a cot while the big man tapped, scrutinized, listened, and performed some eye tests. "Follow my finger. Good. Can you hear this? Feel that? Fine. You're all right, but a candidate for about twelve hours' sleep. Better go to bed as soon as I leave. I'll be seeing you again very soon."

"Any word from Lake House?" Indio asked.

"Fallon's calling out the Guppy militia. Big uproar. You'll be visited by a team of amateur sleuths tomorrow. Be nice to them, boys."

"What about the nurse who helped me?" Evan asked. "Will she be all right?"

"They'll question her, naturally, but we think we've left enough false leads around to take the heat off her."

"When can I see her?"

"See her!" Buzz laughed. "What an idea! You were in grave danger, we saved you, and now you want to go back and visit a nurse! You might as well know, Evan, that she's a clone, and not interested in young men."

"You're wrong! The others may be zombies, but Eliza —"

"Never ceases to amaze me," the physician marveled. "Human beings can always find some positive aspect in an impossible situation. However, it so happens that you're partly right about Gamble. I did the workup on her, and I agree — she's different. Little quirk on the environmental side, probably. A woman named Gamble gave birth to Eliza from an implanted cloning egg. They let the woman and her husband raise the child, and maybe she picked up some romantic ideas from them. Dunno."

After he left, Indio and his friend set up a cot, and Evan, reeling with fatigue, stretched out and immediately fell into a sleep like death.

When he awoke, he felt better than since he was

103

reanimated. He stretched and looked around the little dirt-floored room. Although the air was hot, the sheet-iron shutters were still closed. Corky was writing in a notebook. He saw Evan sitting up, and looked at him.

"How do you feel?"

"Better. Don't you want some air in here?"

"Can't open the shutters. They act as scramblers. Indio and I will be going to the mess hall in a few minutes. You can't go there yet, but we'll bring you something."

Indio ran in from a back room. "Company coming!" he whispered. "Get into your clothes, and put this mask on. It'll fit like your own skin. It was made while you were still half-frozen."

Evan could hear men's voices and grating footfalls. He pulled on the jump suit, while Indio brought a decal of a tiger's face and slapped it onto his shaven scalp. "This is a head decal," he said. "A lot of young guys are wearing them. Hurry up!"

Outside, a treble voice cried, "Open in the name of the law!"

Fists thudded on the door.

Evan pulled on the mask. It fit perfectly and was as light as a spider's web. He had a glimpse, as he donned it, of a coarse face with a scar on one cheek. Indio opened the door.

Four old men stood outside in gray uniforms with red armbands. Behind them, Evan saw a bleak field of black cinders, where windowless buildings smoked and trucks moved about. The tallest of the men, who appeared to be about eighty, but was still free of the Guppy taint, stated with authority:

"We're here under the Omnibus Seniors Search Law!"

"Think of that!" Indio said.

The old man looked at a photograph he held, comparing it with the faces of the young men who stood before him. It was a picture of Evan, taken while he still had hair.

"Names?" he barked.

They gave their names, but although the photograph did not resemble any of the boys, the searchers continued to stare at them in suspicion.

"Why aren't you out with a truck?" one man demanded.

"Because we work nights."

"I'd better check their P.I.N.s," said the leader, gruffly. "You fellows go on to that long dormitory. Somebody just peeked out the window."

"Right, Harold," said another of the old men. They marched away.

The tall old man closed the door and sighed. "Poor old dears," he said. He offered Evan his hand. "Evan, you can call me Pop. We don't have much time, so listen close. You'll ride the truck for a day or two, maybe a week, depending on how things go. Here's your identification booklet. Your picture's in it, so always wear the mask in public."

Evan looked at the booklet, and shrugged. "You know all I really want?" he said. "To get out of the city and back to the redwoods. Can't you work that? Once I reach the woods, I can live on the land till it's safe."

"That's not going to happen for a while, my boy. You might have to hide out for years. Right now all our timetable includes is a little alteration to your memory."

Evan grimaced. "Got any ideas for doing it without making a zombie out of me?"

"If all we wanted was to destroy your brain, Evan, you'd still be in Clark Memorial — stiff as a mackerel. Trust us."

Indio and Corky went to the mess hall for breakfast, then to some classes they were required to take. Evan stayed in the stifling shack. The mask was comfortable enough, and he kept it on. The mirror revealed that Stan Tully was ugly, slow-thinking and surly. His identification booklet recorded that he was a habitual runaway, had tried to bomb a Rejuvenal center, spent six months on a correctional space-island, and had only recently been paroled to the garbage facility.

Evan memorized the important points and looked for something to read. He found an American history book with a chapter on his family. He lay down and began to read.

"Three great events stand as beacons in the history of mankind," the chapter opened. "The discovery of fire, Koch's pioneering work in bacteriology, and Clark's discovery of Rejuvenal. . . ."

He skimmed, snorting now and then at some nonsensical bit. ". . . The family was a close-knit one, and in the evenings might be observed chasing butterflies down Main Street for Evan's collection."

Then a sad recital of misfortunes, starting with Evan's disappearance and ending:

"At last the final tragedy struck. On a motor trip

only a few years after the government's approval of Rejuvenal, the family's 'camper' was struck by a logging truck on a winding road near Crescent City. The Clarks were instantly killed. . . ."

As Evan closed the book, he felt a mooring give way in his mind. He had known they were dead, but now he felt adrift in time and space, an ancient mariner, a time nomad. Every cell in his body was a product of Ferndale, 1984. But that town and that century were embalmed now in records and gravestones. He wished his parents could have known that he had not suffered, had not been murdered. But Hawkins had let them grieve, and had launched him on a voyage through time, to land on an alien planet, where he had no family and no friends, except for a girlfriend who had evolved into a monstrosity; and, thank God, a nurse-clone who was some kind of behavioral aberration.

He wished she were with him now.

*A*t four o'clock they left the dormitory, checked out a garbage truck, and Indio swung it onto the road leading from the refuse complex. Other trucks came and went in the dusk. In the distance Evan saw lines of stubby space capsules on what Corky said were laser launchers, ready to embark for that big garbage pit in the sky.

Beyond the walls and blue-green hydroponics fields lay a few hundred acres of conventional farmland. The agricultural belt was soon behind them, and they entered a zone of small factories with narrow rooming houses wedged among them. A woman trying to wrestle a trash barrel onto a curb screeched at them, but Indio passed without slowing. The woman shouted and threw a rock at them.

Evan began recognizing buildings, and realized

they were in the Harley Mansions area again. He looked around, irrationally hopeful. Eliza worked nights now, so it was unlikely that he would see her shopping among the pushcarts.

"That nurse — isn't this where she lives?" he whispered.

"Be quiet."

The truck wriggled through a block of vegetable barrows and small shops, then suddenly halted, settling to the street before a reeking garbage pit at the mouth of an alley. Indio jumped down, pulled on gloves, and handed Evan a shovel.

"Do what we do," he muttered. "Don't act too bright."

They began shoveling refuse into the carrier. Shopkeepers rushed up with last-minute buckets of refuse. A big man in a dirty smock walked up.

"Bring a bucket down the alley before you leave, mate," he told Indio. "Some clod dumped his slops in front of my door."

"Get a bucket and do it yourself."

"Don't have a bucket. But here's my card."

Indio pulled off his glove and pocketed the twenty-Clark bill the man was offering. "Go with the man," he told Evan. "When you're through, carry the bucket out the far end of the alley. We'll be at the station there."

Evan had already recognized Buzz Baker, the physician who had checked him out last night. He followed him down the alley. A young woman peered out a window at them. A man sitting in a doorway with a bottle of pink gin did not even look up. Buzz hauled out a ring of keys and began unfastening padlocks.

"It's inside, actually," he said, opening the door to reveal a room below ground level.

Evan entered behind Dr. Baker, who closed the door and said, "Now! Out of these clothes and into those on the cot. I've got a slider waiting."

Evan pulled off his uniform and unfolded a white jump suit. On the left breast pocket he saw a logo of folded hands, and the words: *Lazarus Society*. He shuddered.

"But that's where I started!" he protested. "In the deep freeze! You're not putting me on ice again, are you?"

"No, but there's surgical equipment where we're going — everything we'll need. In an hour, Evan, it will all be over. Pray for time!"

21

Eliza had been told to be ready to leave her flat at oh nine hundred hours, but it was fifteen hundred before the knock came on her door. The cat growled and bristled. Remembering that the vicious little Rodriguez had killed her last cat, she shut him in the bed alcove before opening it.

But it was not Rodriguez. Four men in black uniforms stood in the hall. "Let's go, Gamble," one of them said. . . .

There was a swift ride through corners of the city she had never seen before, ending in an oxygen dome that rested like a derby hat on a hilly portion of land. The men never uttered a word, even in reply to her questions. They treated her like a captive, not as a nurse who was going to assist Dr. Corday himself in an operation on President Fallon. They entered the dome through an air lock and floated down a broad

111

street to a small lake, at one end of which was a building that resembled a mausoleum: the famous Lake House, the presidential mansion.

"Have they learned anything about Evan Clark?" Eliza asked, as they stopped before the building.

"Stay with the slider," one of the guards said to the driver.

"Right, sir."

She wrinkled her nose at the guard. Oaf, she thought. They stood a moment before the building, waiting. To Eliza, Fallon's home looked like the Lincoln Memorial. She was curious to see what it was like inside. On the small lake there were swans and ducks, and a sort of gazebo from which music floated. It was lovely, but seemed much too splendid for such impoverished times. The chief guard must have received a signal, because he started moving up the steps.

"Move!" he told her, sharply.

Again they waited, before a bronze door in a marble wall. It rolled aside and they entered a vestibule. The security man pressed a button. Without warning, the walls disappeared — simply vanished. They had turned to glass, with only a hint of reflections. They were looking at a vast floor plan, like a doll's house. A central hall split the building into business offices on the right and suites of living quarters on the left. In the administration section, dozens of men and women were at work, with only the arrangement of furniture to show that they were actually individual offices. Some were on talkers, some rushed from cabinet to desk to console with papers in their hands. It was like looking into a beehive with glass walls, where each bee went frantically about its duties.

Most of the living area was empty. She saw collections of furniture arranged as salons and bedrooms, a huge kitchen where white-clad cooks worked at tables, counters, and ranges. There were two sumptuous dining rooms, and in a rear area there was a small surgical theater. Eliza saw an impressive room where the president himself sat at a desk. General Rodriguez was there, too, and Dr. Corday lounged in a chair, the elegant madman. But all of them were watching the visitors in the vestibule.

Fallon touched a button and his voice echoed in the corridor. "Come in, Gamble. Straight back and through the last door on your left. You may leave, guards."

The walls began to cloud, but before they became opaque, Eliza made out an ominous little group in a room near Fallon's office. She uttered a moan. There, in the chairs, were Captain Tuggey; Head Nurse Jansen; Brumitt, the night security man, his elbows resting on his knees and his head hanging — and four security men.

The smoky walls went solid, and she shivered and suddenly wanted to flee. "Go on!" her guard said sharply.

Eliza walked down the hall in her pink coverall carrying her nurse's case. She felt terrified and very vulnerable. Her rubber soles squeaked on the polished marble. She pressed the button beside the door. It opened and she was looking into the president's office. The three men regarded her blankly. Rodriguez beckoned. She entered and stood in a red square on the floor, five meters from the desk where Fallon sat.

"It's late, Mr. President," she murmured. "I'd expected —"

"We've been busy, Gamble," said Fallon, his crystal eyes glittering. "Corday's already done the work on my orbs."

"Oh, so you don't need —?"

Rodriguez took the case from her hand, glanced into it, and said:

"Shall I bring in the others now, Mr. President?"

"Get her a chair, Corday. Yes, bring them in."

Corday moved a chair from its place against the wall and seated Eliza near the desk. The seat was too shallow, and the back was tilted forward. She was wretchedly uncomfortable. Fallon continued to stare at her. Two security men brought in the ratter, the head nurse, and the night guard, and left. Brumitt uttered an angry sound and pointed at Eliza:

"She did it! She's the one!"

"Brumitt!" Rodriguez reproved. "As you were —"

"Sit down," said Fallon. Eliza wanted to look at Tuggey for reassurance, but did not dare. She caught a mere glimpse of him in a knitted metal shirt and chromed casque; so he must have been working when they picked him up. She was conscious of Jansen sitting upright, rigid as steel, could hear her uneven breathing.

"Hello, Eliza!" said Tuggey, cheerfully. "How's the cat?"

"Never mind the cat," the president said. "We have evidence that Evan Clark is dead."

"No! Oh, no!" Eliza whispered. Tears flooded her eyes.

"That's asinine," said the ratter.

"Captain Tuggey!" Fallon struck the desk with his palms. Everyone looked at him, astonished. Eliza noted professionally that the blood vessels in the clear aspic of his face were like red threads. "Explain yourself, Captain," he snapped.

The exterminator looked amused. "Why would they have gone to so much effort to kidnap him, only to murder him?"

"Our evidence is that they attempted to etch the information from his brain, but botched the job and destroyed him."

"I see. . . . Then you have him back? You must, to know all this."

Fallon swiveled his receptors at Rodriguez with a tiny rasping sound, and Eliza knew he was lying. She went weak with relief. The security chief, wearing a gold medal on his black uniform, walked to the desk and sat on a corner of it. He slipped a case the size of a deck of cards from his breast pocket.

"I'll bring them up to date," he said. "Let them know where they stand." He punched a button on the instrument, and a viewing screen glowed on the wall behind Fallon. Suddenly there was a motion picture, in three dimensions, of Captain Tuggey walking toward the entrance of Clark Memorial Hospital. The picture zoomed to a close-up of his face, and froze, as he waited for admittance. Words streamed across the screen above his head.

TUGGEY WILLIAM H 94867204 MALE 43 YEARS INDICTED SUBVERSION 2/21/60, 1/19/61, 5/5/63, REL'D INSUF EVID FINANCIAL WORTH EST + 1 BILLION CLARKS (NEW) . . .

"A game," said Rodriguez. "We're going to do a little odds-making. There's some fascinating information on all of you in the files." He pressed several keys.

"And I find the likelihood that you, Captain, were involved in the kidnapping comes in at" — digits streamed across the screen and were totaled — "930:1000."

Tuggy laughed. "Bosh! A child's game."

"You were there! On the night Evan vanished, you were on the roof."

"In the presence of Head Nurse Jansen."

"Which gives *her* a probability of —" There was Jansen's cold, thin face as she slipped her ID card into the slot before the hospital entrance, a racing line of information about her, and then the stream of figures and a final equation: 746:1000. Jansen rose, her face the color of tallow.

"It's not true! Not a shred of —"

"Your alibi is the ratter's word, his alibi is yours," Rodriguez pointed out.

"There is the log, witnesses in Valhalla, Eliza Tertia's word —"

"Whose own probability of guilt stands at —" The face, the information, the final equation: 978:1000.

Eliza wailed. "That isn't right! How can you believe I conspired, when I fainted when I found Evan missing? Did you feed my physical signs into the machine?"

"Go on, Rodriguez," said Fallon, grimly.

Rodriguez punched several keys, and the figure 356 shone on the screen.

"Ah! She's innocent!" Rodriguez announced, and chuckled.

"You see!" Eliza cried.

"But, consider the fact that chemicals could produce such a physical reaction; then add the meaning of your having willingly ingested such a substance — Now the figure is 909 — And add your vital signs *at this moment —*" Readings which Eliza understood (blood pressure, pulse rate, hesitancy factor, respiration rate) flashed on and off. "And finally we have — 1000!"

"But what about the guard?" Eliza protested, looking around.

"Oh, Brumitt's been cleared. He passed all his tests with flying colors, except a simple intelligence readout, which says he's a moron."

Brumitt scowled, glaring at his folded hands.

A bell chimed. Words poured across the screen. Fallon raised his hands for silence and turned to study the message.

REFUSE SCOWMEN NOT YET LOCATED. TWO LEGITIMATE PAROLEES THIRD POSSIBLY IMPOSTOR. DR. LIONEL "BUZZ" BAKER BEING SOUGHT SO FAR LEADLESS.

"Anything to add, Captain, that might clarify things for us?" Fallon asked cheerfully.

"No. What's this about scowmen?"

Rodriguez lifted a small box from the floor behind the desk. "Oh, you didn't know? Here are some artifacts we found in an alley near the hospital last night."

He held up a springy mass of fine black thread.

"One filament of synthetic black thread. Three half-kilometers of clear synthetic with two-quintal test! Several pulleys. Evan was lowered from his room to the alley, from which he was carried away. There was no vehicle in the alley last night except the regular refuse scow. The men who operated it are known as Indio and Corky. Their truck was found this afternoon, abandoned, near an oxygen stand owned by Doctor Baker, who used to work in Clark Memorial."

"What's that got to do with me?"

"You were in Valhalla last night and there are marks on the roof parapet today where pulleys were installed."

"But he was with me!" Jansen protested. "Helping with a vacationer who had, er, fainted. Captain Tuggey just happened to be handy when I got the call to come up."

"Such a rash of faints," said Dr. Corday. "So we can say: *certainly* Tuggey, *probably* Jansen, and *more than likely* Eliza Tertia. I've been thinking about you during the re-an on Evan Clark," he said to Eliza. "I know you scored highest of all the Eliza clones on gerontology work. But I've never heard you express exactly how you feel about the Guppy problem."

Eliza tilted her chin, but her voice quavered. "I don't call them Guppies, Doctor, and I don't regard them as a problem."

"Of course they are. Especially to themselves. Don't be coy."

Eliza looked down.

"You've taken care of more of those disgusting Logardo cases than any of your sisters. But I notice a recurrent word in your final reports. *Released*.

'Patient was *released* at 1324.' *Released*, Eliza? In all cases, you meant 'died.' Do you look on death as a friend rather than an enemy?"

She felt as though her finger had been pricked but she must make every effort not to bleed. "I look on it — when a patient is — not interested in — in continuing to live —"

She hesitated, then heard herself rambling on in a sort of reverie. "I had a pitiful little old man last month. I liked him, and did everything I could to stimulate his interest in living, but he just languished. And one night I asked him, 'Don't you *want* to live, Jimmy?" And Jimmy said, 'Of course not. I've been around the barn too often — a thousand times too often.' "

Fallon leaned across the desk and glared at her, but she ignored him and went on:

"He explained that there were no more surprises and no more challenges. No hope, no useful self-delusion."

"Did you record this?" Fallon asked, angrily.

"No. It didn't seem important."

"As a nurse," Dr. Corday rapped, "I should think you would know that what a patient says and what he means are often two different things."

Eliza knew she was convicted; but, remembering the Committee of Thirteen, she no longer cared. They were all cruel and selfish, and needed an injection of truth.

"Jimmy meant it," she said. "He meant that you can prolong life, but after it has ceased to have meaning, what's the point in living? How long can you go on doing the same thing, hoping and being disappointed, without giving up? So many of them have said to me, matter-of-factly, 'What do I have to live for?' If a lot of people didn't feel that way, why would we have Suicide Bingo and Valhalla? And the Logardo epidemic?"

Fallon struck the desk in fury. "Without hope? They have everything to live for! They can travel. They can — play games."

Eliza laughed, brazenly. "Games! And who pays for their ridiculous games? We Juvies! They're drones! And the ones who aren't drones have all the decent jobs, as well as the good living space. While people under sixty live in — in kennels! I know — and yet I've got two rooms all to myself, because of my specialty."

"Goodness, what eloquence!" said Dr. Corday. "Nevertheless, there *is* point to their existence —"

Eliza noticed that they all spoke of Guppies in the third person, but she went along with the practice. "*What point?* Can they fall in love? Have babies? Raise them, work at their jobs, dream of success, develop their talents? Nonsense! They've done all the living that they're ever going to do, and now they're just waiting for death. But if they can't even hope to die, then they're as helpless as those poor heads in the Committee room. . . ."

There was a stunned silence. Clocks must have stopped all over the country, she thought.

"Oh," Corday said drily. "You've been up there."

"Yes. It's absolutely revolting. Insane."

Rodriguez pressed a button. The door to the guardroom opened, and four security men strode in. The general spoke to Fallon.

"We have more than enough to hold all of them, Charlie, except Brumitt. The only question is where."

"I haven't decided about Jansen," Fallon said. "Confine her somewhere, and continue questioning."

"It isn't fair! I'm faithful!" Jansen sobbed.

"As for Captain Tuggey, I consider him a very dangerous man, probably the head of the Juvenile Underground. Solitary confinement for him, and encourage him to tell us more."

The guards moved in. "Sure that's what you want, Charlie?" the ratter asked. A guard produced wire-thin handcuffs, and the ratter extended his hands, smiling.

"What's so funny?" Rodriguez asked.

"I was thinking of the plague of vermin after my Pied Pipers go on strike."

"They'd better not!"

"They will. I have a half-million exterminators across the country, and I exert total control over them. In case of my death or disappearance, no one lifts a hand."

"That is a threat!" Rodriguez shouted. "Mr. President, that is treason."

Tuggey kept his hands extended. "It's a fact of life, Rodriguez. Have you any idea how many rats we trap in the course of a day? Enough to make tons of high-protein food for my armies of cats and dogs. As for ants, mosquitoes, roaches, and houseflies — they're measured in carloads. Take my word for it, the air will be solid with insects!"

Fallon stood up. "I won't be intimidated! I'll nationalize your organization!"

"With volunteers? I'd like to see that, Charlie; I love comedy. They'd be torn to shreds by my animals. They really aren't pets, Charlie. Most of them are absolutely savage with strangers. As for insects, I have my own equipment for dealing with them, and of course it would be destroyed in the event of any emergency. Like mosquitoes, Charlie? Rat droppings in your food? Then go right ahead."

Eliza recalled a time when she was a child, just after pesticides had to be banned, because the oxygen-generating plankton in the oceans were on the verge of extinction. Her mother or father would stand guard while the others slept, to kill the rats that threatened to bite them. She remembered the hurriedly issued state swatters, useless against the clouds of flies and mosquitoes. And the mice, the roaches — opening a cupboard door and seeing them covering everything edible.

Soon after that dreadful interval, hundreds of exterminating firms came into being, most of them to be taken over finally by Captain Tuggey's force, men and women organized like an army and devoted to the man who paid them the decent wage they were denied elsewhere.

Evidently the others remembered those years, too. It was quiet in the office, and finally Dr. Corday cleared his throat. "Do you want my opinion, Charlie?"

"What's that, Corday?"

"I think we should give him a little time. During which you might consider nationalizing his firm. At the moment, he might be of more use to us outside than inside."

"Do run it through your think tank, Rodriguez," Captain Tuggey urged, grinning.

The president sat at his desk and pondered, his wasp-eyes glittering. Then he punched a button and spoke into a microphone.

"Captain Tuggey may leave. Take him back to wherever you picked him up."

"What about the ladies?" asked Tuggey.

"We're holding them until we find Evan Clark and get his story."

"Don't do anything you'll regret, Mr. President," Tuggey said.

22

*L*azarus Society vault number 263 had not been used in years.

Within the low, windowless structure, atomic generators kept banks of compressors turning and its thousand crypts chilled, maintaining guests in at least as good a state of preservation as they had been when they checked in. But as people outside lived on and on, sustained by Rejuvenal, it had become obvious that there was already a population glut, and the advice on the cells, which were shaped exactly like those in a beehive, was ignored: *Waken after the conquest over nephritis . . . leukemia . . . heart disease . . . hypertension.*

The undead remained unliving.

Only a few relatives ever came here. And because the Lazarus Society vaults never required tinkering, Dr. Baker had chosen one for the work he had to do.

124

Wearing official coveralls and carrying toolboxes, they briskly climbed the steps to the door. Evan had noticed that people on the walk frowned at the emblems on their breast pockets, and looked away, uneasily. Inside, a central aisle ran back between high tiers of cells. The cover of each cell was of triple glass, with a bronze card below it and a tray for flowers. With a shudder, Evan looked in at the sleepers. Their faces looked as hard and white as marble; their hands were folded, their eyes closed. Most of the sleepers were quite old, but some were children, and he saw one infant.

"Is that the way he looked?" he asked, queasily.

"Afraid so. Better than most, since you hadn't been ill."

"What happened to Doctor Hawkins?"

"Killed himself. Remorse, maybe. Didn't bother to tell us about you, though. Here we are."

He stopped before a door, unlocked it, and they entered a large echoing room like a laboratory. The walls were white, the floor dark green. There were morticians' tables, tanks of gases, skeins of colored tubing, and wheeled stretchers.

"*Voilà!*" he said.

Several chairs were grouped near a mortician's table. Buzz indicated one and Evan sat down. The doctor sat also, facing him.

"I'll be brief," he said. The procedure I am about to perform is known as a cortical peel. You may know that memories are not embedded in specific areas of the brain — they're distributed all over the cortex, the outer rind of it. And they sink deeper every day."

"So you're going to skin my brain."

"In a sense, with low-power laser — a sort of fog of intense light. That machine over there — the one that looks like a hair dryer of your day — is the instrument I'll use. You won't feel anything. You'll probably talk a blue streak as I stimulate certain memories, all of them recent. You'll talk about Eliza, and the food at Clark Memorial. And then about where-are-you, and there may be some bad times as you relive your first waking moments after the re-animation. Then we'll go a micromillimeter deeper, and you'll probably remember Doctor Hawkins. And finally — I hope — the other day in the lab, with your father. Other memories will be intertwined with it, and to remove it cleanly would be like plucking a single strand out of a steaming kettle of spaghetti without disturbing the other strands."

Evan nodded. He was cold and shivering.

"When we have reached this level," Buzz said, "and I hear you voicing recollections of your father, and Methuselah the rat, and other things that happened that day, I'll know your father is about to dictate his recipe for immortality. Then I'll boost the gain a little, and the memory will be etched away."

"And Eliza? She goes, too? And you? Everything I've experienced since I came to?"

"For a while there will be a slight mist over those memories, but I'll control the depth of the etch very precisely. You'll remember me, but perhaps not my name at first. And definitely you'll remember Eliza!"

Evan relaxed. "Well, I guess you want to get started."

"I think we'd better."

23

There was a sort of barber's chair in one corner, where the laser cone rested on its stand. Buzz seated Evan and adjusted padded head clamps.

"No pain, no convulsions," he said. "You may feel a slight prickling of the scalp. In fifteen minutes it will be over."

Evan wanted to moisten his lips, but his mouth had gone dry. He tried to speak, but had no voice.

"No strain, no pain," Buzz murmured, rolling the machine into position. "You'll feel like talking. Let it all out so I'll know how deep we are."

The dome descended. A green light filled the inside of the machine. "— When you begin to remember what your father was dictating, try to refrain from speech. If you repeat the process aloud, then I'll have it in *my* brain!"

Suddenly Evan heard himself speaking.

" *'Worry about yourself, not her. . . .'* "

"When was that?" murmured the doctor.

"When we reached the shed last night."

"Now a little deeper."

" *'. . . I'm walking out of here tomorrow,' I told her, and she said, 'No, Evan, you must stay for a while. Best medical help —'* "

"And deeper . . ."

"Eliza said, 'Captain Tuggey gave him to me. He's over the hill for ratting. . . .' " The scene unrolled in his mind like a television drama. He could see the dark-haired nurse in her baby blue coverall holding the tiger-striped cat in her arms. Then it was gone, and scenes formed and twisted out of shape like visions in water; rose to the surface smoothly, swirling with color and emotion.

"And still deeper —"

" *'So clumsy of me,'* " Eliza said. The film zipped along faster. " *'Well, sweetie,' Eliza said, 'you were found by rangers in . . . in an old missile silo . . . and brought here. . . . He got millions of names on petitions, and they made it legal for human beings to be stored — sick people. . . .'* "

He heard Buzz breathing, very close to him.

". . . I can see the meadow in the woods. Hawkins' place. No! You rotten — get away —!" he cried.

"Now, just a tickle further —" Buzz murmured.

" *'— Vitamin B. I hear it's good for charley horse, Evan. Although if you didn't jog so far —'* "

"Who's talking, Evan?"

"Dad."

"I have to, to stay in shape for practice." Tears

came to his eyes. "He was really a great guy, Doctor. . . . If he'd had any idea —"

"Aren't we about there, Evan?"

It was right after breakfast when he told me about vitamin B, and then said, 'Moose, I want to show you a rat that's going to make Methuselah look like a chump. There are side effects to Rejuvenal, but this new drug. . . .' "

In his dream he saw them leaving the breakfast table and going down the stairs to his father's basement lab, and heard loud voices — yet somehow they were not part of the scene. His mind seemed painfully sensitive, picking things up and tasting them for emotional flavor like bits of candy; but there was a bitter taste to his mind, now, and fear.

Harsh voices. "Back away slowly, Doctor. Slowly. Hands high. Keep talking, Evan. Everything's all right — don't worry."

In the dream he was having — for it was exactly like the sleeping visions one had — he saw himself and his father in the lab; his father was turning on a tape recorder. Yet he also saw several men in black coming into the lab — the lab he and Buzz were in — holding tubelike weapons. And Buzz was shouting:

"Don't talk, Evan! They've come! Don't say it —"

But he could not waken from the laser-induced dream; it had more tangibility than this nightmare of the Lazarus Society vault, perhaps because he wanted to believe in the past, wanted to go back. People were standing around him, and Buzz was lying on the floor. Another voice was speaking to Evan, and he rolled his eyes and saw the troutlike, always-in-powder-blue form of Dr. Corday, sitting where Buzz had been. The icy skull came close.

"What a nice surprise, Evan. Go on with what you were saying."

"I don't understand, Dad," Evan murmured. *"It's the same process? 'No,' he said, 'you didn't follow me. The process in Rejuvenal consists in sealing the cell walls so that Protein XY, let's call it, can't leak out and cause the cells to age and die. But it's imperfect; protein continues to leak away. Substance 1000 not only seals the protein inside, but chemically restores lost protein! In other words — the cells, and the body, become young again.*

" 'If I were a gold miner, Moose,' he said to me, 'I'd shout, Eureka! And yet — and yet — I have doubts.' What about, Dad? I said. 'About the wisdom of hyperlongevity,' he said. 'Four hundred years of crossword puzzles might grow a bit tedious — tedious for the person paying your bills, too. Well, as a scientist I suppose that's not my concern. Are you going out to Hawkins' today?' "

"Got it," said Corday, exultantly. "Got it, Rodriguez! Got it! Stars and galaxies — we've beaten them!"

Evan rambled on, distressed. He saw Dr. Corday writing on a scratch pad, chortling, and Rodriguez pounding his back. Then Corday seemed to remember Evan, and turned off the machine, and down he came, like a hot-air balloon in flames. With a thud he landed. He was in the Lazarus lab, and Buzz was sitting on the floor with his back against the wall, dazed. General Rodriguez was speaking into a talker on the wall.

"Well, put me through to him. Tell him I said, *Utmost!* Of course he'll understand!"

Two of the men in black rolled away the machine, and Evan stood up, staggering, utterly drained. He spoke to Corday, but the surgeon did not seem to comprehend. His features were filled with what, for him, probably passed for emotion.

"I didn't catch that, Evan," Corday said.

"I said, where is Eliza? Eliza Tertia?"

"Oh. Odd you should ask! We were talking with her just a while ago. She may be at her flat by now. Why don't you go see? The address — Rodriguez, what's that nurse's address?"

"Harley Mansions, Eleven Iowa Street."

"You mean," Evan said incredulously, "that I can go? I'm not under arrest?"

Corday laid a palm on Evan's shaven scalp. "No, son, we've got what we wanted. But stay in touch. You'll need money, and Charlie will help you get set up in a nice apartment somewhere — you're a very wealthy young man. Thank you. We'll put you on the hundred-Clark bill!"

24

*E*van paced the corridors of the vault, feeling as though he had slept too long, and was having trouble getting his mind back in gear. He was aware of a deep anxiety, a shadow of dread. He went back to where he had left Dr. Baker lying on a high wheeled table. The doctor had told Evan where to find a certain pill in the stores, and had taken it without water.

"Are you okay?" Evan said.

Baker opened his eyes. "Oh, galaxies, Evan!" he groaned. "For another five minutes! Five minutes!"

Evan massaged his neck with both hands. "I tried to hold it back, but it just rolled, like a movie. Maybe they didn't get it all. Maybe we should finish up, in case —"

"They got it all. I could hear you, even if I couldn't move."

"So they'll rush into production on it —"

"Immediately. It's the same formula as Rejuvenal, with a change they can make in their existing stocks. And then it will be hey, nonny nonny, dancing in the streets and long lines at the Puncture Pavilions."

"Is that thing on the wall a telephone?" Evan asked.

"Telephone? Yes, I suppose it is, though we call it a talker."

"I want to try to call Eliza."

"She wouldn't have a talker. There's a shortage. But we'll go by her place. Chance in a thousand, but — Give me a hand, eh?"

Evan assisted him, and Buzz sat up and muttered, "I can see now why they call them stunners!"

"Can you find her place?"

"Oh, yes; yes indeed. We've kept an eye on her ever since we learned from Jansen that you were at Clark Memorial. She was a main key in our plan. But, Evan, I want you to be prepared for a disappointment. Few clones speak the language of love."

Evan shrugged. No use explaining again what he felt when he was with her; that his electricity was a direct response to hers, that the current was alternating, running from him to her, from her to him.

"Maybe you could walk now," he suggested. "We probably don't have much time."

He helped the doctor down the corridor. Outside, in the rusty sunset, they found the Lazarus van where they had left it. They got in and set off, dodging through an industrial area and finally entering a neighborhood of cluttered residential buildings. Evan began noticing activity on the walks. People were running, or clustered in groups. They reminded him of scout ants along a disturbed trail.

"It's out," said Buzz. "Charlie Fallon's probably been on television."

In a Guppy district, an old man in a hat like a beekeeper's bonnet waved at them and shrieked: "They've found Evan! Oh, Minerva! We're going to be young again!"

Through an air lock they went from pine scents to the fusty odor of poverty. Buzz drove fast, frowning. The street began to look familiar, tattered blocks of four-story wooden structures a couple of centuries old. Evan perked up. They were in the Harley Mansions neighborhood.

The doctor parked suddenly, set locks and burglar alarm on the van. They were in front of number 11. Elephant Plan graffiti were everywhere, and on the steps stood a gathering of men and women. He heard them talking about Evan Clark, although they obviously did not recognize him. And a good thing, he reflected, or they might have torn him apart. The doctor picked a way through the congregation and they entered a musty lobby. There was a long, dim, lower-floor hall, a staircase at the right. Buzz led the way, climbing wearily. Evan pushed past him.

"What apartment number?"

"Twenty."

"A nurse lives in a barn like this?" Evan looked at the numbers on unpainted doors.

"Oh, this is Class-A housing! Professional people. She has two rooms and doesn't share. And just a cork pop from a gin mill."

They found the door, armor-plated and with no visible lock. Evan pounded and listened. "Eliza? Eliza!" There were sounds from other flats, but none from hers. He knocked again, then tried the knob. The door swung open.

"Of course," said the doctor. "They probably took her away and didn't bother to lock it after themselves."

It was a dismal little flat with no rug, a window looking out on a brick wall, a toilet stall opening directly off the parlor. There was an alcove with a bed, a battery-powered stove to its right, and one closet. But the flat smelled faintly of Eliza's perfume, and there were small, pathetic decorations — an abalone shell, a stuffed quail she must have found in a pawnshop, several water colors of fruit — a pronounced emphasis on food in her decor.

"Maybe she left a note?" Evan said.

Dr. Baker pretended to help him look; he was clearly without hope. In the closet Evan found a surprise: a model of his home in Ferndale. It was complete even to carpeting, furniture, and tiny miniature books in half-inch-high cases. Buzz leafed through an album of pictures of members of the Clark family, while Evan investigated the bed alcove. A magnificent cat regarded him from the pillow. A tinny voice said:

"No use, fellows. Come to my place. Bring the cat."

The cat looked startled.

Behind Evan, the doctor sighed. "That's Tuggey. Let's go."

They drove along a crowded street in the Piccadilly area. Merchants were closing their stalls, covering their carts. There was a reek of cabbage and hot grease, and Evan saw people cooking over small tin stoves on the sidewalks, among sleeping mats and footlockers. The doctor swung the van down an alley which ended in a brick wall. He spoke into a transceiver.

"I have Evan Clark here, Pop. I'm going on to my place. . . . Evan, don't take it too hard. Things will look better tomorrow."

Or worse? Evan waited while he backed the Lazarus van, spun it, and charged away. He heard gears grinding, and a section of the brick wall slipped aside. Inside a dimly lighted room he saw an old man — was it the old fellow who had headed the security squad at the refuse plant? He stood blinking at him, a weapon in his hands.

"Get inside," he said. Evan entered and the door closed. "So they wiped us out," sighed the guard. "Saint Vitus rattle their bones."

"Somebody must have ratted on us. They were there two minutes after we started."

"Go on inside, son. The boss is waiting for you."

Evan passed through another door into a small vestibule, heard locks clicking, and realized he was, for the moment, imprisoned. An eye goggled behind a peephole. Then another door opened, and he entered a reception room at the end of a large living room. A big man with brigand's mustache rose wearily from a sofa. He came forward, smiling, and gripped Evan's hand.

"Bill Tuggey, Evan. Remember me?"

"Your voice, I think. All that human-fly stuff, Captain! — and they got me anyway."

Tuggey stretched. "At least they left the head after / they stole the memory. So no regrets, Evan."

Evan gripped his hand. He knew the easiest way would have been to kill him in the hospital — no risk, no chance of a slip-up. But that wasn't the captain's style. "Thank you," he said.

"We're following up on that little nurse. Their problem is that they don't know how dangerous she is. They know she was part of our plan to smuggle you out, but they don't know for sure where she fits into our other plans. So they may hold her for a while — question her, I suppose. . . ."

Evan had a disturbing vision of glaring lights and sharp instruments, and he winced. But the captain said quickly, "Nothing clumsy, I'm sure. They've got their formula, and I think they'll settle for that rather than risk retaliation from us if they hurt her. They'll probably lift her nursing license, drive her into push-cart work like Buzz —"

A pleasant-looking old lady came in, wiping her hands on an apron. "Bless your heart, Evan! You must be starved. I have something you'll like in the oven for you. And Bill, you've *got* to do something about the calls! Every line —"

"No business calls tonight, Mom," said Tuggey, yawning.

"But there are operatives all over the country on hold —"

"Good place for them to be while their tempers cool. Let's eat. Then Evan's going straight to bed."

In the morning there was an old-fashioned
breakfast prepared and served by Mom, who
seemed to Evan to be playing the role of a
nineteenth-century grandmother in a play.
She urged second helpings on them, scolded them
for talking business while they ate, and although
the ratter told her not to worry about them, Evan
sensed that he drew a certain comfort from her
fussing.

Afterward Tuggey spoke to Pop over an intercom.
The conversation was in code. Evan did not understand it, but immediately afterward the big man led
the way to a storeroom and opened a door like that
of a bank vault; inside there was nothing but an
elevator car; at least he thought it was an elevator,
although there was not the least sensation of motion
after the button was pressed. But when the door

opened again, they were facing a small room paneled with electronic equipment.

Tuggey motioned Evan to a chair, seating himself at a desk bare of anything but a cylindrical telescreen. He opened a drawer to reveal a complex arrangement of keys. He thought a moment before pressing in a combination of numbers and letters. The holoscreen came to life, so that the three-dimensional little scene appeared to be taking place in miniature on the desk blotter. A haggard-looking man at a kitchen table was scribbling busily on a manuscript; he removed his glasses hastily as a bell rang.

"Morning, Shrike!" Tuggey said. "Sorry you had to wait. How does your battle plan read?"

"The idea here is keyed to street traffic," the man said earnestly, holding up a much-revised diagram. "Nothing moves, you see. Nothing! No one enters a building, no one leaves, no vehicles move one centimeter. In three days they'll be begging to talk terms."

"Hmmm. How do we accomplish all this?"

"The table of organization is by zones and squads; mobile brigades in the sectors. On the street level, crowd-stunners, nerve gas, earsplitters, and tanglefoam —"

"It's got merits, Shrike. But it's premature."

Shrike looked pained. "Premature, Captain! It was overdue ten years ago!"

"Keep smiling, Shrike. I like it. Send me the details." The picture faded, and Tuggey fed another combination into the control panel and another diorama materialized on the desk. This time it was a young woman in a blue one-piece garment with the word *Sanitation* over the breast pocket. She was playing a game which seemed to be three-dimensional chess. As the ratter spoke she started, causing several of the pieces to topple.

"Hello, Sandpiper," the man said.

"I tried and tried to reach you —!"

"Other people are still trying. What's the plan?"

"Food supplies! It's beautiful! Boost our own minimum basic to three months'. Then all public stores of food will be infected with *Proteus virulis*."

"Never heard of it."

"Yes you have, but you don't always read your messages," Sandpiper said. "Variation of Lassa fever. Our biochemists' own creation — requires intensive care, continuous transfusion, and deep medical back-up. Five cases would tie up a large hospital! And it's highly contagious."

"Oh, fine! So we all get sick together, Sandpiper?"

The young woman grimaced. "Of course not! Vaccine is ready — it gives protection in two days."

"I like it. But I'm filing it under Measures, Final. Send me samples for testing."

"But Captain —!"

"Good-bye, Sandpiper. Falcon, hello."

A young black man was working on a model of what looked like a spacecraft. He pushed the work away, and snatched up a folder. "Our idea should be in your cipher room. Do you want to read it and call me back?"

"Rough it out for me."

"Coordinated strikes on every Puncture Pavilion in the country. We hear Substance 1000 requires a second dose at a certain critical interval. They'll need all their inoculation facilities to accomplish this."

"I'll get information on that. I'm not sure it's true. Anyway, it's premature, and would invite retaliation before we're ready to move."

"Ready to move!"

"I get the impression," the ratter sighed, "that I'm talking into a barrel. No Falcon. Not yet."

He set up another pattern of buttons and the picture changed to the words: ALL STATIONS. "Refine your plans for another two weeks. Then communicate. We've waited years; a few days more won't stop us."

He leaned back in the chair, massaged his scalp, and grinned at Evan, who had been watching with fascination. "Well, young Clark, let's get you fixed up. Money, slider, fast woman to make you forget about Eliza."

Evan smiled wryly. "I'll settle for money, slider, and Eliza."

"Let's start at Lake House. President Charlie, your benefactor."

He talked to a series of executive assistants, and finally the lantern-jawed, smiling head of Iron Eyes materialized, like that of one of the Committee of Thirteen.

"Good day to you, Captain!" he said heartily. "No hard feelings, I trust? Why, you've got young Evan Clark with you! Good morning, Evan."

Evan muttered something but the ratter did a pensive little balancing trick with a pencil and said:

"Evan is under the impression that he has some money coming, Charlie."

"Oh, absolutely. He has assets in all major money depots. I'll issue orders at once to liquidate them. That do it?"

"He also has a yen to visit his old home — now the Clark Museum."

"Get the boy a slider — one of the models with all the toys young people love, eh? I'll take care of the rest."

Tuggey punched out. "Would you believe he issued orders last week to decapitate you? Let's go shopping, Evan."

In the ratter's yellow sport slider, they cruised to Dome Seven, where, he said, all the good stores were located. They floated down a broad, tree-lined avenue under the soiled heaven of the 0-2 dome. Along the way they saw Guppies puttering about the interminable task of time-killing, some playing lawn games, others strolling with colored poodles, others standing on corners as if waiting for something to happen.

"Terminal boredom," said Captain Tuggey. "They're in Fat City, as you used to say. But look at them."

"What happens if Substance 1000 works?" Evan conjectured. "If it really rolls back the clock, then they'll all want jobs again, and more of everything they've already got. And what if they're able to have children again!"

"Please, Evan! Must we talk business? Let's just say that population reduction now has top priority. Here we are — General Slider Corporation. Think you'll like their Sigma Nova, though it may be a little stuffy for your taste."

A courtly silver-haired man wearing too much powder base sold Evan a little red sport van. It had a driver's seat of genuine leather, and ample space in back for a sleeping bag and supplies. The body was of clear plastic, which could be lightened or darkened by rotating a dial. Evan gave his name and that was all that was needed.

Tuggey led the way to a couple of stores where Evan bought food and camping supplies, which many citizens, those who lived on the sidewalks, used for ordinary housekeeping. Then he took him to a bureau where he was issued an identity card, a metal wafer the size of a business card. A Greek alpha was engraved on it.

"Use this for all purchases," the official told him. "The alpha signifies special treatment. If you should ever find yourself in a queue, simply present your card. You'll never wait when you're carrying one of these."

While Evan looked the card over, the ratter said, "And give the boy a sequencer to the Clark Museum in Ferndale, via fastest, with manual stop options."

The clerk programmed a microfiche from a machine, and they left. Tuggey showed Evan how to insert the little card into the auto-control slot of his van.

"When you're ready to leave, push the red button and sit back. It will take you out of the city and up the coast to Ferndale. It will ask questions now and then, such as whether you want to stop for a picturesque view. Push the Yes or No button when it does. And take this," Tuggey said, handing him a tiny transceiver. "You can always reach me on it."

As Evan put it into his box of supplies, Tuggey gave his elbow a squeeze. "Don't hang around there too long. It might be depressing. The world is out here, now. So unless you want to go back into the deep freeze, you'll just have to climb aboard."

"I don't want to be a bore," Evan said, "but what about Eliza? Can this fortune of mine buy private detectives to track her down?"

"You've got all of my people on the job already. Why not let it ride until you get back?"

Evan peered into the amber eyes. "Haven't you ever been in love, Captain?"

Tuggey chuckled. "Oh, Evan! What a nice, old-fashioned term. And yet," he said, "my first wife and I had a certain special feeling for each other that went beyond the practical, I suppose. But you see, when people get 'married' now — well, for example, a young man has freehold to a quarter of a cellar. But he needs a nice set of basic housekeeping supplies. He finds a young woman who owns a set, and they get married. If they don't get along, they trade around with other young couples until it works out. What was the term in your day? 'Marriage of convenience.' "

"How many times have you been married?"

"Eleven, I think — no, twelve. I was forgetting my first wife, because that one didn't work anything out except a sort of mutual need for each other, you might say."

"That's quite a lot, at that." Evan sighed.

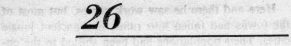

26

*T*he trip north was a trajectory rather than a drive. The slider rushed along at a speed of 350 kilometers per hour, according to the speedometer. There was no road as such. Between walls of brush ran an invisible magnetic lane over which the red van zoomed like an artillery shell. There were turnouts, and occasionally the Sigma would veer to the side to allow a speeding southbound vehicle to pass. There were announcements from a concealed speaker describing a historic spot or picturesque view.

Evan was astonished at the abundance of undergrowth and the height of the trees. Yet plant life, of course, thrived on the carbon dioxide of the impoverished atmosphere. Now and then he saw tree farms, in rows as regular as cornfields, all the trees neatly spired and of exactly the same height. He suspected that they were clones, like Eliza.

Here and there he saw work camps, but most of the towns had fallen into ruins, like ancient jungle cities. Their populations had been shifted to the cities. San Francisco, like Los Angeles, was a bleak specter of dead city areas and bulbous domes reminding him of water blisters. There was no ship traffic and the sea was a weak yellow green, like a leak deprived of sunlight. The Golden Gate Bridge looked as antique, now, as London Bridge had in 1984.

The slider curved on through rolling hills, past hydroponics farms with enormous buildings where luscious fruits and vegetables, said the speaker, were "processed into the dehydrated forms that keep indefinitely and are more easily handled."

The road climbed through a mountain wilderness near the meadows and forests of his home country. He was almost there, now, and his nerve was going. Am I ready for this? he wondered. Would the house have velvet ropes and a guide? Could he take the depressing changes?

The road left the redwoods, crossed the Eel River, and at last, lush and green on both sides, there lay the meadows of home. On a slight rise he saw the silhouette of a small town: Ferndale, where the whole disaster had started, innocently enough, in his father's laboratory.

The van riffled the tall grass of the meadow as it passed. No lovely dairy cows grazed here now. Were they raised in some kind of cell, if at all? A boxy tour slider approached, and Evan's van swerved onto a turnout to allow it to pass. It was full of sight-seeing Guppies, heading back to the city after a day in the wilds. They had made their pilgrimage to the home

146

of Walter Stevens Clark, probably had bought plastic busts of Evan's father to put on the mantel.

The van slowed. Ferndale was small, a few hundred homes skewered on a crooked main street. Things did not look so different, except where trees had grown to giants or had fallen. Even in Evan's day, the village had been a gem of Victorian architecture, where one could neither change nor demolish a building without permission of the city council.

Some electronic intuition in the slider's control center deduced that he would want to gawk a little, and the van slowed to a crawl, creeping up Main Street. The old business houses looked like steamboats gone aground, frosted with wooden scrolls, spindles, and fretwork. There was a railed walk where a few superannuated sightseers in the custody of a guide trudged along, gazing at the ice-cream parlor, the drugstore, the hotel, at Malcom Cameron's Realty. They took pictures of each other. Yet they hardly glanced at Evan, the greatest curiosity of all. A dinosaur from 1984.

The van halted where the pavement ended at a cross-street. There was a dirt road ahead, climbing a hill, and narrow lanes running off to right and left. His home was a block to the left, opposite a church. The recorded voice said: "There will be a one-minute delay for visual diversion. Do not leave the vehicle. Touch nothing. You may take pictures."

Nevertheless, Evan got out and leaned against the van. He imagined Eliza beside him, curious about everything, the little specialist in Old Ferndale. He would point and say:

"That's the Wildcat Grade, Eliza. The logging trucks used to come down it. Beyond those hills

147

there's a meadow; that's where Hawkins had his place. The lab was in an old missile silo. Let's go see my house, now. . . ."

There was a lump in his throat. It would only be a shell, for the heart of his home had suffered a cardiac arrest; there were no odors in it now, no voices, no pulse of life. He tried to understand that fact clearly, so that he would not break down when he walked in. His parents, the nucleus of his world two weeks ago, had been dead for nearly two hundred years. He was not going home, for there was no home to go to. He was going to visit a museum.

He heard the talker in the van rattling, and got in. ". . . At the next corner, opposite the church," it said. "Please remember to remove your headgear when you enter. This is a national shrine. Stay behind the velvet ropes and obey the commands of the ranger, a qualified student of Clarkiana."

And yet the house did not look much different. Having been built of heart redwood, logged out of nearby forests, it had resisted rot, and was still painted a glistening white with yellow and avocado trim. Between the cracked sidewalk and the shrubbery was a narrow strip of lawn. The house was two stories high, with a porch the full length of the lower floor. As a little boy he had ridden a trike on the veranda when it rained. Later he had sat there in deck chairs with Sherrill. He had mowed the lawn every week. He had grown up here, lived here until two weeks ago.

Two weeks, plus one hundred and eighty years.

An old man in forest green opened the screen door and stared at him. "Come right in," he invited.

"You are welcome to visit, providing your credentials are in order."

Evan went warily up the walk and climbed some metal steps superimposed over the old wooden ones. The ranger had a transparent nose the shape of a pale root vegetable, and looked earnest and rather helpless. His shoulder patch bore the likeness of Dr. Clark.

"Yes?" he said, betraying a little impatience. (What was this ignorant boy doing here?)

"Hello," Evan said. "Would you believe I lived here, ranger?"

"No jokes, if you please. I've heard them all. This is a holy place, a national treasure."

"And I'm one of the treasures. I'm Evan Clark."

"Oh? I knew another boy once who was named after Doctor Clark's son. Your sequencer, please."

Evan handed him the card. "I mean I really *am* Evan," he said earnestly. "It's been on the news."

The guard looked at the sequencer, then frowned. "Er — the real —?"

"Yes. I just came to visit my home."

Suddenly, as though Evan were a general, the ranger saluted. "Yes, *sir!* If I could just see your alpha card — because you see —"

. . . The old man checked Evan's credentials in some sort of scanner, then returned them to him. There were tears in his eyes. "Evan, Evan! Bless you! And guess what I just heard on the news! Doctor Corday has started production of Substance 1000!"

Evan wilted. "It didn't take them long to get it out of my head and into a test tube, did it?"

"They're very efficient." The ranger offered his hand, gripping Evan's with his cold claws. "Do you know, sir, I just missed being your friend by thirty years? I was born here in 2001! We might have been pals — is that what you called it?"

"Yes. Pals. Buddies."

". . . Then we moved to San Francisco, and I lived there a hundred years or so — I'm 163 — but I came back when I had a chance. Pardon me, but do you remember what your father said Substance 1000 would do? How successfully it would change us?"

Evan peered past him into the gloomy interior. "No, I really don't. Oh, he said he'd have to test it on rats and monkeys for years, I think. . . . So you lived here. Why did you ever leave for the city?"

The ranger smiled sadly. "Ambition. I had a career as a travel agent. But the exchange rate finally dropped so low that Americans couldn't travel anymore, so . . . Then I got on the ranger list. Say! I'll be going to San Francsico for my Big Shot next week — that's what they're calling it. I can hardly wait!"

"What will you do after you're young again?"

The yellowish eyes reflected, and he looked puzzled.

"Don't quite know. . . . Wouldn't want to work again, except — something like this. I might remarry. Don't know. Probably not. Anything you do too long gets boring, you know. Well! I mustn't keep you, Evan! You know the way, ha-ha! Just stay behind the cords, eh?"

He sounded preoccupied, a bit disturbed. There was a shadow in his eyes, as though some distressing idea had struck him. Evan walked into the house.

It was the wax dummies that did him in.

There was a family group eating plastic steaks in the dining room. Evan, in wax, was a laundered version of himself — the boy hero. His mother wore a benign smile, the perfect mother, and his father seemed to be reflecting solemnly on some very weighty problem. They bore no resemblance to the family that had sat around the table so many times. They had been deified, like George Washington in the picture of him crossing the Delaware. But they brought the tears to his eyes.

With a stony face, he climbed the stairs to his room.

A red velvet cord prevented him from entering, but he could see himself lying on the bed in a football uniform, reading a book. There was noble vision in the boy's glass eyes as he studied Roger Tory Peterson's *Field Guide to Western Birds*. The original furniture had apparently been replaced after his disappearance, but his parents seemed to have kept certain treasured things of his: a rattlesnake's jaws and fangs he had painstakingly reassembled from the skeleton; a red-tailed hawk hanging from a thread near the ceiling.

He drifted to his father's study, at the end of the hall, where a dummy was at work before a rolltop desk. Evan sqeezed his eyes shut to control the tears. For it was not his father at all, merely a grisly sentimental effigy.

Now he knew in his gut that when he walked out of here that day, he had as good as fallen off the planet. There was no place in the world for him. But Charlie Fallon had promised him a few acres in the woods. He would try to come back and live as a hermit, after he found Eliza — and he would! — for she belonged in his world, too. They would live as settlers, go to town only when they had to.

". . . Was there something?" It was the ranger's voice, from the head of the stairs. "You were so quiet."

"No, thanks. I guess I'll go now."

The guide gave him some brochures explaining the town, the family, and Rejuvenal. "I wonder where I could camp," Evan mused.

"Well, you know the road to Centerville Beach. It's only a few kilometers. There's no camping allowed, but naturally I'd want you to make yourself comfortable there. For heaven's sake, though, don't go in the water! It's terribly cold, and very treacherous."

27

*I*n a windy sunset, he made camp on the beach. A half-mile offshore a gray fog bank hovered. The clammy Ferndale summers had not changed. Even the long, featureless beach was little altered, except that there was no trash, no barrels, no picnickers. On a cliff a short distance to the south he saw the ruins of the old radar station.

He made a quick bird check, and saw a few sandpipers and willets; far fewer than in the old days. They ran along the surfline drilling for sand crabs betrayed by the retreating water. Not far offshore he saw the black heads of several seals. The surf was too rough to bodysurf, but he'd do it before he left.

He spread a plastic tarp, laid out his bedroll, and set up the tiny cooker which resembled a canned-heat stove of his day. He opened a packet of compressed beef stew and put the grains in a pan with water. In two minutes it was steaming. It had little flavor, even less than the hospital fare, but at least it served to kill his appetite. He ate, then sat watching the sun descend into the fog bank.

He thought about Eliza.

It was curious that they should have held her, since they had not detained Tuggey. Of course they were afraid of Tuggey, who might turn all his Juvies loose. Thinking that, he heard a muffled voice in his pocket, and pulled out the little transceiver.

"Hello, Evan! How does Centerville Beach look after one hundred and eighty years?"

"Not too different. How'd you know I was here?"

"Myron, your ranger, reported in to Charlie, and a friend at the Communications Pavilion passed it along. Everything all right?"

"It's a long story. Oh, I had one idea. How many people knew Buzz was going to use the Lazarus Society vault for the work on my memory?"

"He did, Pop did, and I did. Certainly none of us told on you."

"Who got the Lazarus uniforms for us? Maybe he could have doped it out."

"Pop got them, days ago, through a friend in the network. Nothing that will ring bells there."

"Then how come they knew right where and when to come? Coinicdence?"

"Possibly. Some of the Society vaults have brain scanners on hand for initial stimulation in reanimation cases. Maybe they fed *scanner* into the machine, and that popped out. They must have known he'd be using some such type of equipment."

"Right. . . . And yet the way it happened — right on the dot — there's *got* to be a fink," Evan said. "That head nurse, Jansen?"

"Jansen's dropped out of sight, too. She was my main operative at the hospital. She brought in the rats. She even got me into Valhalla to rig up the pulleys. Jansen is pure gold."

"She treated me like a department store dummy."

"How else could she treat you and not get caught? Brumitt's one of our people, too, but he didn't know it."

"Hmm. And you feel sure it wasn't Pop? He's an old man; maybe when he got to thinking about being young again it was too much — asking him to destroy his only chance."

"He's an old man, but one with a young man's philosophy: 'No heroic measures.' And he regards artificial prolongevity as a heroic measure. In fact, the Elephant Plan was his idea, and he refines it in all his spare time."

"What is it? I saw some Elephant Plan graffiti on buildings when I was on the garbage scow."

There was a pause. Had Tuggey been walked in on? The small, hard waves thumped on the sand. The water was lead gray, with creamy foam. The ratter's voice resumed.

"It's a plan for easing people out when it's time to go. There was an old legend that when it was time to die, elephants wandered into the forest and just vanished. Valhalla is a form of life-limitation that the Guppies developed themselves. A happy death, an easy death . . . But Pop wants to systematize and dramatize it. He's playing with an idea whereby persons near the cut-off age go to a lively wilderness area like you're in right now, with a group of others about to die. They'd have death workshops, group talks, music. . . . Well, it's a long way off. Anything I can do for you?"

"Send me that little bottle of perfume from Eliza's flat. It's called Remembrance. I'll use it as bait, like fox scent, and dream her out of hiding. . . ."

He found a little driftwood and tried to build a campfire, but either the shortage of oxygen in the air or the slight dampness of the bonelike sticks doomed his efforts. He crawled into his bedroll, slept, woke to find himself engulfed in mist, snuggled deeper, and slept again.

28

For several days he took walks, jogged, and swam. He felt the old Moose coming out of hibernation in his bones. He threw rocks at the water, swam out beyond the surfline, bodysurfed back. The cold water stung. Much of the time he still felt a little tired, and decided it was the atmosphere. He was running an oxygen deficiency.

He visited the museum again, and Myron, the ranger, said:

"I've got a present for you!"

It was the bottle of perfume from Eliza's flat! Tuggey had sent it up. He sniffed it and the tightness in him melted. He could almost hear her voice.

"I'd like to ask a favor of you," Myron said. "Would you mind staying here while I go to the city for a few days? I get my Big Shot tomorrow!"

157

"Sure."

"There won't be any visitors. All the Puncture Pavilions are working around the clock! Doctor Corday took the first injection, right on television! Oh, and guess what? I may bring back a surprise!" He crowed with glee.

Evan looked sharply at him. Eliza! Had Charlie decided to turn her loose? Send her up to him? Why not? He punched Myron's shoulder; it felt like sticks inside a bladder of aspic.

"You'd better have a surprise! I need one," he said.

He did not actually believe it, but it was going to be a terrible disappointment now if Myron did not bring her back.

He spent several days in the old house. No visitors came. He cooked with his camping gear, slept in his own bed, the dummy on the floor. For exercise, and since it helped to allay his anxiety, he jogged through the streets of the town, from the Fig-Twig Dance Hall down to the Veterans' Lodge; then north to the fairgrounds, and south into the meadow where small creeks gurgled.

He heard from Captain Tuggey one night.

"I'm glad you don't have to watch it. They're giving young-again parties in the streets; just gin bashes. But I get the impression nobody's having much fun somehow. . . ."

The next day, in a small room Myron apparently used as his personal cubbyhole, Evan found a television setup. It consisted of a frosty-looking panel on the wall, and a remote-control dial. He pressed a button and it came to life.

There was a street scene, which he recognized because it was directly before the hospital. People were doing some kind of square dance. Many were drinking. There was so much noise that he could scarcely hear the voice of the reporter. What was striking was to notice, on close-ups, that the Guppy effect was fading from the old faces! And it seemed to him they were growing taller; or, more likely, simply acquiring better posture.

The dancing was frantic. Yet, as Tuggey had said, no one appeared to be having much fun! There was something driven about the celebrants — contorting bodies, somber faces. They reminded Evan of the Hans Christian Andersen story about the girl in the red shoes, who danced herself to death because she could not stop.

"The drug works, no doubt about it!" the reporter cried. "Look at those happy Seniors! And as you know, the only untoward effect of this substance is that the translucent flesh is being replaced by a — well, you could say an *aluminum*-colored skin."

Evan watched television now and then over the next couple of days, and one morning Myron came back in a gleaming purple slider. He rushed out. Sure enough, there was a woman with the ranger! He ran down the walk, shouting and waving. As Myron got out, the other door opened. Myron moved spryly; his flesh was no longer transparent, but of a thicker consistency, like that of an aspic laced with aluminum filings. The old man swept his arms around and cried:

159

"Meet the missus, Evan!"

Evan halted. It was not Eliza, but a woman in a lavender wig who looked about seventy, although probably she was much older. Her features were mannish, but she was dressed in pink overalls with lace trim.

"Hello, Evan," she said, coming around and taking Myron's arm. "It's such a pleasure."

"This is Ruth," said the ranger. "Knew her when we were kids. We decided to tie the old knot."

When Evan had recovered his voice, he said, "Congratulations. Ruth is the surprise, eh, Myron?"

"You betcha," said the old ranger. He reeked of alcohol, and a collection of plastic swizzle sticks protruded from his overall pocket.

"Well, well. I hope you'll be very happy," Evan said. "I'll move my stuff out."

"Don't bother," Ruth said. "Myron has this cute little place right on Main Street, and we'll live there. This place here is just a museum," she sniffed. "Stay awhile. Can't he handle things, Myrie?"

"Sure thing. I want to show Ruth the countryside, Evan. Come on, kiddo! Let's go."

Evan was reminded again of the story about the red shoes, as they sped off.

. . . He saw them occasionally as they rushed by, waving; gradually he settled in at the house. He took down some velvet ropes and rearranged his bedroom the way he had had it. He stored all the dummies in corners with tattered sheets over them. He turned up some ancient fishing tackle in the basement. The line had hardened and could scarcely be peeled off the reel. The hooks were rusty, but he cleaned them. In the meadow, he dug worms, and then started fishing in a winding stream.

When he caught a trout, he noticed that its gills had slightly more flare than usual. Aha! he thought. An evolutionary adaptation to the shortage of oxygen! In time people's chests would probably deepen and the ribs flare, like those of Peruvian Indians at extremely high altitudes.

He studied the fish as it lay on the damp grass. He had read that one reason scientists believed it was wrong, and difficult, to extend life beyond reasonable limits was that nature required a certain number of generations to perform her evolutionary changes. In ten eighty-year generations, she could accomplish *something*, at least, in adapting a creature to its changing environment. But in one eight-hundred-year generation, she could accomplish nothing. The creature simply died, if the environment outgrew it.

This fish was many generations removed from the one he used to catch here. So the species was adapting. But man could not.

He cooked the fish in an old skillet of his mother's. As he ate on the veranda, the transceiver rasped.

". . . Corday's sick!" Tuggey's voice said.

"What?" Evan stood up, shaken.

"Charlie Fallon said he'd been in an accident; but we don't believe it. Buzz thinks he's getting a delayed reaction to Substance 1000! The palace guards came for Buzz, to help with Corday. Despite being on their bad list, he's still highly respected as a physician. Maybe you'd better come back tomorrow."

Another voice overrode his. "This is a bulletin on

161

the UEF, utmost emergency frequency. Evan Clark, are you there? Evan Clark, are you there?"

Evan held the transceiver near his lips. "This is Evan Clark."

"Return at once. You will be stopped automatically at the north Golden Gate station for a new route sequencer."

"Get stuffed," Evan said, knowing the voice: It was General Rodriguez on the air.

"What was that?"

"I won't come."

"You have no choice. You are needed in extremely sensitive work. Leave at once."

"I'm not leaving until you come up with Eliza Tertia Gamble. Bring her here and I'll cooperate."

"You have no choice!" Rodriguez said.

"Yes, I do, and I'm not leaving. I know this country and you'll have to find me."

A pause. "We can't give her to you because we don't have her."

"What happened to her?"

"We turned her loose that day, and she hasn't been seen since."

"Then find her! There may be some more secrets in my head, but you'll never know until you produce Eliza."

He put the instrument in his pocket and ran into the house. He collected his camping things and rolled them into a sort of backpack. He did not know how far away the nearest security policeman was, but he hoped he had time to make it to the hills. For what did people know about tracking in this day and age?

He left the slider before the museum and crossed the street, turned west at the hotel, and trotted up the dirt street that became the Wildcat Grade. He leaned into the slope as he jogged, past the Fig-Twig, where he used to go to dances on Saturday nights, on into the woods. Through ferns, rhododendrons, and fir seedlings. Panting, he climbed toward the first low ridge.

From there he looked back over the village. He saw a large silver vehicle rushing toward Ferndale. It entered the town and headed straight for the Clark Museum. Three men in the black garments of Rodriguez's special police sprang out. They inspected Evan's slider; then, stunners drawn, charged the house. Evan turned his back on the town and descended a hillside into a shallow valley. Then he started climbing the next timbered ridge.

29

*T*hat night he lay on his bedroll in a tangle of manzanita. He had eaten some of the compressed food, and now watched a blanket of mist roll in from the sea.

He had seen no pursuers. Tuggey had not called him again, nor did he respond when Evan tried to tell him what had happened. But suddenly he heard another voice saying:

"You have nothing to fear. The Committee of Thirteen is already on the job. In the meantime it is suggested that all persons who have had the injections take a saltwater enema and drink large quantities of fluid. . . ."

A moment later a different voice said: "Twenty-ten medical advisory. Disregard all previous advisories. Emphasis is on transfusions. Persons experiencing symptoms of this disease, which has been given the name of Cryptoplasmic Amorphosis-X, or CAX, are advised to avoid alcohol and take moderate exercise."

He listened for an hour, heard people ordered to exercise vigorously, to avoid exercise, to shun alcohol, to take three centiliters of gin every hour, to call their physicians, and to refrain from jamming the airways.

He heard a call requesting volunteer ambulance drivers.

Doctors were summoned to the Clark Memorial Hospital poison center.

Nurses were instructed to report to Central Nursing.

Then a jolly newscaster suddenly said: "President Charlie Fallon announced today that over ninety-three percent of all seniors have received the injections. Within a week, all remaining persons over eighty will have —"

The bulletin was chopped off. Another voice said: "Please ignore the foregoing accidental rebroadcast. . . ."

He slept, and woke to see that the stars were out. Over the transceiver he heard a man saying gloomily:

". . . so that they may be collected more easily. Repeating, please place at the edge of the sidewalk the remains of any individuals who have expired in your home, so that drivers of collecting vehicles will not have to enter the premises. It is now believed that the epidemic may be of a contagious nature and unrelated to Substance 1000."

In the morning he prepared something called Phase A, which proved to be a concoction suggestive of overcooked scrambled eggs. While he was eating it, he heard Fallon's voice calling his name.

"I hear you," Evan said.

"We've found Eliza Tertia!" the President said. "She wants to speak to you."

Eliza's voice said: "Please come back, Evan."

He scrambled up. "Eliza!" he said. "What happened in my room that morning?"

"What morning, Evan?"

"The morning you told me why I was being held at C.M.H. Why did you agree to tell me?"

"You — you persuaded me."

"How?"

"With your gift of gab. You sweet-talked me, as they said in your day."

"Liar," Evan said. "Who are you — Duodecima? Sexta?"

"Really, Evan! I heard that they needed you, and as a humanitarian gesture I came back."

"What's unusual about the Committee of Thirteen?"

"— They're the outstanding biochemists of our day."

"Anything else?"

There was a sound in the mist overhead. He looked up. An airship shaped like an egg was descending toward him. It crushed the manzanita beneath its runners as it landed ten feet away, and two men jumped from a door. Evan ran, but a stunning force hit him in the neck and he fell. Paralyzed, he lay facedown on the earth.

"Sorry, Evan," someone said gruffly.

30

The next thing he knew, he was sitting upright in a seat beside a window of the aircraft, wearing a black jacket. There were three security guards in the cabin with him, one of them at the controls. He did not seem to be under restraint, but when he moved, he felt air hissing into long chambers in the jacket, and the taut fabric held him absolutely immobile. When he relaxed, the air hissed out and the pressure eased.

"Take it easy, Evan," one of the guards said. He was a sturdy old man with ears sticking out like the handles of a jug.

"What's going on?" Evan mumbled.

"Quiet," said the pilot.

"Report," a voice said through a speaker.

"Coming in."

"Destination now Lake House. *Utmost!*"

The guards looked at each other. "Great Galen!" the pilot muttered.

Evan looked down. They were passing over San Francisco Bay. He could see the sea's pea green arms inside the Golden Gate. Ten minutes later, as they crossed a desert, the guard with the protruding ears said:

"Is this that first-abe — first-aid — that — um, kit they gave us?"

The pilot looked sharply at him. "What's the matter, John?"

The guard was pawing futilely at a plastic box. "I feel funny — there's a ringing in my ears —"

"Here —" said the third guard, who opened the box. All Evan could see in it were some tubes of pills. The man shook a couple onto his palm. "I'll get some water. . . ."

. . . And then there were two, thought Evan. The man was only half-conscious, and seemed to be swelling inside his black uniform.

"When did you have your Big Shot?" the pilot asked the other guard.

"The same day he did. . . ." Then he turned in anguish to Evan. "They're going to ask your help, son! Why won't you tell them what you know?"

"Because I don't know anything."

"But you were there!"

"The stuff hadn't been tested. Or," Evan conjectured, "maybe this is what Dad intended it to do. Give people a few spectacular days, and then — He erased the tape," he said. "He must have had some reason —"

"What *possible* reason?" the pilot groaned. "I mean, it was cruel, selfish —"

"How'd you like to have the power of eternal life in your hands? Who gets to live? Who doesn't? What happens to people after five hundred years of croquet? Do they get wicket-happy? Invent Suicide Croquet, or Musical Chairs with one of the chairs wired for twenty thousand volts? Maybe that's why he did it. The responsibility —"

The pilot mumbled, as if in a daze, "Charlie Fallon says there is never a right time to die. Death is a violation of God's — how does it go, Arthur?"

"On the other hand," Evan said, becoming interested in the subject, "man himself is only an experiment. They say human beings have been around for two or three million years. Seems like a lot, huh? And yet the dinosaurs were regarded as a failure, and how long do you think they lasted? Two hundred and fifty million years! Some failure! Compared to us, they were as successful as the housefly."

The guard groaned and gazed at the landscape below. In a few minutes Evan saw the mountains north of Los Angeles rising from the valley. There were yellow hills, then green forested ridges, and a series of valleys. A bell rang and they were over the vast congested metropolis, with its domes, greenery, dead cities, and boulevards. The pilot let the craft settle toward earth as it flew on, then homed in on a small dome, like a bee going toward a hive. There was a red-rimmed opening in the dome, and they dropped through it before it closed. They held at a hundred dekameters.

Evan saw something that startled him.

In a grassy park among flat-roofed buildings, there was what resembled an army on maneuvers, row upon row of bodies facedown on the grass. A few upright figures moved among them. At one side of the square was a line of vans; workmen were hauling bodies to them and loading them inside.

"What's that?" he asked the pilot, feeling squeamish.

"That's an evacuation station," the man said. "I hope you're proud of yourself, Evan. Those are bodies being moved to the space-scow station."

"What for?"

"To be disposed of. To avoid possible contamination. They're being off-loaded in space scows. . . ."

They dropped softly, like a child's balloon, upon a mausoleumlike building before a small lake. Uniformed figures hurried about a parking lot. The guard unzipped Evan's straitjacket and pulled it off. Evan looked at the man who had been taken ill, and shuddered. His face was aluminum-colored and moonlike.

The aircraft settled upon the lawn surrounding the building. Several guards ran up. On the steps waited a black-clad dwarf — General Rodriguez. A door lowered and became a ramp, and Evan walked out.

Rodriguez shouted and beckoned for haste.

The pilot and the remaining guard hustled Evan toward the building. Rodriguez impatiently hurried them inside. They started down a wide hall. At one side a man in a powder blue uniform lay on a stretcher. Evan did not immediately recognize him, but Rodriguez muttered:

"Corday won't be of much help to us! He had the first injection — one day before me and a few hours before Charlie Fallon."

170

He opened a door and motioned Evan inside. Evan was now in an enormous bedroom with blue-and-pink Persian rugs over a white marble floor. There was a raised bed under a canopy. Lying on it was Iron Eyes himself. He lifted his head to look at Evan. His face was a dull metal color somehow more in keeping with his black orbs. He looked like the figure in the Michelin tire ads, grotesquely inflated. With effort he raised a hand. At his side was Dr. Baker.

"I hoped," Fallon said huskily, "— get things — I'm not ready, boy —"

"He wanted to find that nurse for you," Rodriguez said hastily. "But Corday was the only one who knew where she was incarcerated, and after he was stricken he couldn't remember."

Iron Eyes was mumbling. "— Aides!" he whispered.

Rodriguez said impatiently, "There were some aides with Corday, but all I've been able to find out is that they were from the hospital."

Iron Eyes was mumbling. "— Aides!" he whispered.

"— Ask your help —"

"I *can't* help," Evan said. "You already picked my brain, and I never did know anything about the process. Besides, it would have to be a deal. Eliza, or no go."

Fallon stared at the velvet canopy over his head, mumbling to himself. "World without — world of —"

Rodriguez barked at Dr. Baker, "Get him on life support!"

171

"He's been on life-support for almost ninety-six years," the doctor said. "Substance 1000 was merely the ultimate life-support system, and it apparently has a side effect: death."

"Then reverse it!"

"Maybe Walter Stevens Clark could reverse it. I can't. I'm not even sure why the drug has the paradoxical effect."

"But you have a theory?"

"Everybody's got a theory. Mine is that Substance 1000 causes the cells to synthesize the protein that Rejuvenal lets leak away. The cells are enriched and rejuvenated; so is the body. But the cells don't know how to stop producing the protein, so they become engorged and finally rupture. It's as good a theory as any, but it would take months to prove it."

A bell began to ring, insistently.

Evan looked at the old president, who lay still in the enormous bed. The flesh of his face and hands was softening over the bones. The crystal orbs still sparkled, though the mind behind them was dead.

General Rodriguez glanced at a small blue light in the wall above a door. It beamed and rotated with sapphire brilliance. Rodriguez pulled a chrome device from his belt and spoke into it.

"Colonel Borg? What is it?"

There was no reply.

Rodriguez looked at the doctor. "What's going on?" he asked, puzzled. "That's the final warning light. Do you know why it's on?"

"It's the takeover," Baker said.

Evan heard footfalls in the corridor, and a shout.

"The takeover?" the general said. "Oh, no. It

won't be as easy as that. Lake House is inside the last zone of defense. There are five zones, each —"

The noises were subdued, and yet there was a sense of rapid movement, of many people in the corridors. The doctor leaned over the late Charlie Fallon, studied him, and drew the sheet up to cover his face. Then he turned to Rodriguez.

"Defense," he said, "implies defenders. If eighty percent of the defenders are dead, or defectors, then there is no defense, is there? Captain Tuggey is already in the presidential office, broadcasting the manifesto. There won't be a revolution. There aren't enough Seniors left to put up resistance, because of the efficiency with which you managed the Big Shot."

Rodriguez shrugged. "Well, well. Then there's no point in pretending to resist, is there?" he said. He glanced at his wristwatch. He did not look like a beaten man; his eyes were still bright. He was scheming, now; bartering. Voices were audible outside the door.

"I have nearly twenty-three hours, Doctor," he said. "That's all I need, if you'll help."

"Did you help the Committee of Thirteen?"

"That was Corday's great idea." Rodriguez shrugged. "It's over and done with. I can make you one of the richest men in the country —"

"I told you I can't help, even if my services were for sale."

"Where's your imagination?" Rodriguez grinned. "There *is* a way out — for a few of us. One of them, by necessity, would be Doctor Krueger, the cryonics man. I see you're catching on," he added.

Evan was catching on, too. Hawkins' Principle:

Put a person into cryonic suspension until a cure is found for his illness. Would that apply to enemies, too? Was that why Dr. Corday had brought medical aides to handle Eliza, instead of guards?

". . . It was my escape hatch — my personal survival plan," Rodriguez said. "There's still time, Baker. Nothing irreversible has happened to my body."

"But something irreversible has happened to your political party."

"I've always collected precious gems," Rodriguez said. "There's a strong room that would make your palms itch. Are you afraid of me? Is that it? Ridiculous! 'Never worry about a man on ice leading a coup.' That was a favorite saying of Corday's. All I'm asking —"

The door opened, and several men entered. One of them was Indio. Rodriguez looked at them. "Well, what about it?" he asked quickly. "Krueger is waiting at the vault. . . ."

Evan approached him. He saw that the general was perspiring.

"Is that what Corday said about Eliza Tertia?" he asked. "That you wouldn't have to worry about her if she were on ice? Is that why he brought medical aides that day?"

"That's certainly possible," Rodriguez said. "I wasn't in on it, but it is a possiblity. You'll have to admit it was more humane than killing her. . . . Why don't we go over to the vault and see?"

"Lock the general up somewhere," Buzz Baker said. "Evan and I will go have a look."

31

"W e'll check the directory first."
There was an alcove just inside the
Lazarus Society vault. Evan watched
the doctor insert a cylindrical key in
a receptacle in the wall, and saw a small keyboard
like that of a calculator, each button glowing.

Dr. Baker punched in Eliza's name and serial
number, but only a series of flashing zeros resulted.
He tried her hospital identification number. There
was no result, no indication of whether she was
stored here, or if so, in which of the honeycomblike
cells.

Then he fed Colonel Jansen's identification numbers into the directory, to no avail.

"We'll have to make a search," he said. "I still
think there's a chance."

Only about a third of the six-sided cells were in
use. As they started down the main aisle, he saw that

there were scores of empties. Each cell had a triple glass door and a bronze name plaque.

FOX, ARTHUR H., 39240061. RENAL FAILURE
SAMUELSON, THELMA R. . . .

Inside he saw shaven heads, white as porcelain. The bodies were clad in robes, white for women, blue for men.

Wait!

Wouldn't Corday have separated her from the others? Possibly; but why? He didn't know why; but she was certainly a special case, and might have received special treatment. Segregated from the others, in case — in case what?

They worked along opposite sides of the aisle. The cells were stacked eight high. ". . . I only saw her once," Buzz Baker said; "at Tuggey's one night. There's a chance they didn't shave her head, so we might —"

Of all the Lazarus Society centers in the city, why search this one? Well, they had come here, and probably they'd have stored her here after they finished with Evan. It was logical. Corday had had the aides with him, and Eliza might have been held in the van while they got her cell ready.

He reached the end of the aisle and turned left. There were two other aisles. He skipped the second and went to the last, against the wall, thinking: Maybe he'd have gone for a corner cell — out of sight; less chance of being seen. There was a stepladder at the end of this aisle, but as far as he could tell, all the cells in the area were empty. He used the stepladder to scan the topmost compartments. All were vacant. Then, from a distance, he heard Baker clear his throat.

". . . She had dark hair?"

Evan twisted, but could not see him. "Right! In a bun."

"Maybe you'd better come over here."

Evan dropped to the floor and strode along the main corridor, peering down each cross aisle until he saw the doctor on a ladder in the farthest corner; he was peering into a compartment just under the ceiling. The doctor came down, patted his arm, and Evan climbed, but stopped two shelves below the one Buzz Baker had been examining. He felt shaken, battered by all he had been through lately, not sure that finding her here, frozen, was much better than finding her dead. And what if they had killed them both? Wouldn't they have had to hide the bodies? If so, what better place to hide them than here?

". . . It was a very common procedure, years ago," Buzz was saying. "Success rate quite acceptable. And we're talking now about someone who was in perfect physical condition when she was put in vital arrest."

Evan saw a crystalline rime of frost in the compartment before him; wondered about moisture leaking in. Could that be right?

"There's no sign of violence," said Buzz, reassuringly. "Even if they'd been poisoned, the features would have been distorted. Why don't you look, son? And then we can talk about ways and means."

Evan climbed the last two rungs, his eyes shut; then opened them when he felt tears forming beneath his eyelids. He had to rub his eyes to clear his vision. He stared first at the red-haired figure in the end cell. Jansen's face was like ice, and she was dressed in a white toga. But oh, she looked dead! Lifeless as the woman of ice that she was.

Then, at last, he looked at Eliza.

The petite features were like the finest bone china, without a blush of color, even in the lips; white lips, an artfully carved mouth of ice. Dark, even eyebrows, dark lashes, dark hair frozen slightly askew: the only suggestion of life.

"How many —" he began, and had to start over. "How many of them do they lose?" he asked.

"A few. But morbidity accounted for most of the failures. Don't forget you looked just the same only a few weeks ago. You believe you're alive, don't you? So believe Eliza is."

Evan touched the glass with his fingertips. He felt as though she were a thousand miles away. "How does it start?"

"There's a direct-line talker here. I'll call Lazarus headquarters. Somebody will jump a meter when the bell rings."

"Buzz!" Evan said. "Something funny. There was frost in the compartment below hers a minute ago, and now it's melting."

"Cosmos and Damion!" Dr. Baker said. "I forgot — one of the elements of the takeover involved turning off the power to all Lazarus Society vaults! The cells are already thawing."

32

*D*r. Baker switched off the talker. No one had answered at Lazarus Society headquarters. "Not the best time to try to raise anybody, especially the dead," he said. "The Lazarus teams were all Guppies, and hadn't been called in years, except the team that did you."

Evan could see beads of moisture inside the glass covers of the nearest compartments. "Does the work start here?"

"No. It's a one-way street, here. There's no warming chamber, and no blood for restitution — has to be matched and balanced. There's nothing but Hawkins' Formula, a gas that replaces the liquid in the cells so that they won't rupture when they're frozen. But reanimation has to be done at C.M.H."

"So we need a slider to move them?"

"There ought to be a couple of vans downstairs. That's where the one I had that day came from."

He ran to the alcove in the rear where he had started the work on Evan that day. There was an elevator here, and he pushed the Down button, but nothing happened.

"Damn!" he said. "Apparently only the lights still operate. That probably means the garage door doesn't work either."

They went outside, but there was no switch to activate the door at the bottom of a ramp. It was controlled either from within, or by radio impulse in incoming vans. He led the way back, and began opening cupboards at random.

"Insulation robes. Belts. We'll have to wrap them the best we can and move them to C.M.H. on trolleys."

He found a supply of padded silver robes and they carried these, and a ladder, to the corner. "We'll take Jansen first."

With a ladder at either side of the head nurse's cell, they lowered her, stiff as a board and light in weight, to one of the wheeled stretchers. Dr. Baker began wrapping her in an insulated blanket. Evan hurried to belt her in place.

"Careful," Buzz murmured. "There's danger of, er, chipping — ears, noses, knees, and toes. But we have no time to waste — we don't want any thawing. It has to happen from the inside out, and the transfusing must start almost simultaneously."

They climbed again and slid Eliza from the compartment. She was rigid and pitifully light. All the blood in her body had been replaced with Hawkins' "noble gases," which were weightless, so that she seemed as hollow as a cocoon from which a butterfly had emerged. Evan was trembling; sweat trickled down his scalp, for he knew that if he fumbled she would shatter like an ice statue. At last she was on the trolley, and they wrapped her in insulation robes.

"I'll take Eliza, you take Jansen," said Buzz.

Evan followed him down the corridor to the door, pushing the cart, and down the ramp to the sidewalk. "Can we wheel them like this all the way to the hospital?"

"It's only a kilometer. Maybe we'll find an abandoned van."

Soon they were in the heart of the city's best residential area, Guppy Heaven, but it had deteriorated into something resembling a medieval plague city. A van would have been of little use after all, for the street, as they proceeded, looked like a destruction derby: stalled or floating sliders with the dead or dying inside them; overturned ones; swollen bodies lying on the pavement. A sliderful of ancient Guppies, apparently racing to Clark Memorial, flashed over fallen bodies and crashed head-on with another. People tumbled out, dazed, most of them showing the obvious signs of Substance 1000 poisoning. Colored poodles wandered about, one of them tugging at its dead mistress's sleeve. Across the street, in a parkway, a team of workmen labored to align bodies for removal.

As they hurried on, they stopped to move bodies now and then, in order to push the trolleys past. The eyes stared, mouths bulged open. Evan thought of Civil War photos. And all the time the outside heat was working its way through the insulation robes, to start the process of decomposition. Baker was trotting now, and swearing. Two young people, a man and a woman, emerged from a shop with

181

merchandise in their arms; they stared at them and then ducked into a side street.

A block ahead, Evan saw a shining blue pyramid towering above all the nearby residential buildings. He knew it must be Clark Memorial.

Dr. Baker swore. "Look at that mob! Everybody and his brother crying for salvation!"

There was a shouting horde at the hospital entrance. Many people lay on the walk, but others fought to reach the doorway, screaming, and a half-dozen men and women were hammering at the armor-glass windows with croquet mallets.

The doctor maneuvered Eliza's trolley into a side street. "We'll have to use the back way. I had duplicates made of my keys when my license was lifted."

They hurried along another street congested with stalled or drifting vehicles and wandering, weeping Seniors and their poodles. No one seemed to think it odd that two men should be pushing hospital stretchers down the sidewalk. Buzz pushed the cart into an alley. Evan followed him, panting. Did he imagine it, or was the heat increasing? Had some enormous air-conditioning apparatus been switched off?

At last the doctor halted, and Evan remembered the alley well. Buzz pressed a medallion against a lock, a door slid aside, and they entered the building. The door closed. They trotted down a service corridor until they reached an elevator, where Buzz pushed a button and they waited, panting. The car came and they rolled the trolleys inside. It rose, slowed, and halted; a bell chimed; they pulled the carts into a corridor. On the wall in green letters were the words: LAZARUS ONLY.

They followed an arrow to an echoing, deserted room with a shining blue floor. Along a wall five large glass cubicles were aligned like huge, empty display cases. Behind them was a vast panel of switches, a vascular system of many-colored tubes leading to the reanimation cubicles, a shining jumble of carts, tables, and trays.

Buzz opened the door of what proved to be a refrigerated room, and motioned Evan to help him maneuver Jansen's trolley inside. Evan felt the bite of dry, bitterly cold air. They unbelted the nurse and threw off her insulation robes. Then they went out and opened one of the reanimation boxes. Buzz pushed Eliza's trolley into place and told Evan to stand at the opposite side of the patient. They removed the silver robes and Buzz pulled the white Lazarus garment from Eliza's body. Evan shuddered when he saw her lying nude, alabaster white, on the tray: Small plastic valves were buried in the flesh of her neck, arms, legs, and groin.

"Give Corday credit: He was a perfectionist," Buzz said. "The valves have been installed perfectly and left in place. That's where they withdrew the blood, and it's where we'll pump it in. You aren't going to pass out on me, are you?"

Evan took a steadying breath. "I'm all right. I think I remember a place like this — before I was really awake —"

"Watch what I do, and do the same. Blue tubing to blue valves, red tubing to red. In a couple of hours you'll see her turn pink. It's quite inspiring."

After the connections were made, everything was automatic. They left the cubicle. Evan was trembling, and when Buzz asked him how he was, he could not speak. He was relieved, he was fearful, he was weak.

"I'll make some coffee," Buzz said. "Then I've got to call Tuggey."

"When will she be awake?"

"This is Tuesday? About Thursday. I don't want you to see the shivering and stupor; it won't help her or you. It's all automatic anyway."

The coffee helped, and Evan was cheered when he thought — then knew for sure — that Eliza, decently covered with a reanimation garment, was turning pink: Her face looked so normal that he tapped on the glass to see whether she responded.

"She looks okay, huh?" he said.

But Buzz had a talker in his hand. ". . . Sparrowhawk, this is Weaver. Oh, hell, we don't need code now! Indio, get me through to Tuggey. We're at C.M.H. and we're all right. But he's got to get the anti-looting squads to the domes fast."

They sat there, breathing deeply, sipping coffee and resting. "The calm before the storm," said the doctor. "I'll be surgeon general during the transition period. Didn't want the job, and I'll quit as soon as it seems decent."

"Is there a plan — you know, a takeover scheme —?"

"Plans, schemes, projects, designs, options, alternatives — push a button and stand back! They've been in the computers for fifty years. We have block wardens, zone commanders, mayors, governors, commissions. But human beings are human beings, so we have police, too, and the looting won't last long.

"Then there will be a great silence," said the doctor, "and finally the sound of small wheels turning. Then big wheels, and within a year people will worry again about who they are and what they want to do with their lives. In three years we'll hold the first election. Then we can all settle down to complaining about taxes and worrying about our digestion, not to mention the meaning of it all. And what are you going to do with your life, young fellow?"

Evan looked at Eliza. "Go to college," he said. "It seems kind of unimportant, though, doesn't it? — studying the relation of bugs to animals and the relation of animals to people?"

"Not at all. You might think of the relation of the plankton in the sea to the oxygen in the air — that's where eighty percent of it used to come from. We need a plan for unsouring the seas to enable the plankton to flourish again. There's an international commission working on it, but Charlie Fallon was always so busy inventing Seniors projects that he didn't get around to appointing scientists to it —

"Well," the doctor said, "I've got to get up to the control room and start issuing orders. Will you come along?"

"No, I'll wait here awhile and watch over her. It's the least I can do."

He watched intently for a couple of hours, but suddenly discovered he was falling asleep. He arranged some insulation robes like a mattress and lay down near the cubicle.

He slept for over three hours, according to the clock on the wall, but awoke when he heard a bell tinkle. He sat up. Just something to do with the machinery, he decided. A green light was glowing.

185

Eliza looked quite natural, as though she were in a very deep sleep. He tapped the glass again, but she did not respond.

For a while he sat in a yoga position, observing her closely, alert for the minutest change in her face. Two days, Buzz had said. Another hour passed. He became suddenly aware that he was hungry. He had had nothing to eat for days except that sawdust food of theirs.

He recalled passing a small delicatessen fragrant with gourmet foods. He would go back and steal a few days' provisions. Would it be safe to leave the sanctuary of the hospital? The bloated, dying Guppies might have invaded the alley by now, searching for the help they imagined to be inside. He decided to risk it — at least glance out the alley door. For with an armful of provisions, he could spend the days of Eliza's reanimation right here.

It was important that he be on hand to greet her when her eyes opened. He knew what it was like to wake up cold, sick, and bewildered. Would she smile when she saw him? Cry? Probably both.

All that stuff about clones not falling in love! It was nonsense. He and Eliza would prove it.

About the Author

Frank Bonham was born in Los Angeles and wrote his first short story when he was ten years old. Since then, he has published forty-five novels, twenty-five of which are for children and young adults, and several hundred short stories and novelettes, as well as some television scripts. In fact, he loves to write.

Mr. Bonham is married, has three sons, four grandchildren, and a green parrot named Charlie. He lived in Southern California until recently, when he moved to a small town in Arizona where he continues to write short stories and novels. Among his popular titles are *Gimme an H, Gimme an E, Gimme an L, Gimme a P,* available from Vagabond Books, and *The Rascals from Haskell's Gym* and *The Missing Persons League,* which are available in Scholastic Paperback editions.